D1296252

Deep Water Blues

"Fred Waitzkin effortlessly recreates a singular world with uncanny insight and humor. His language is remarkable for its clarity and simplicity. Yet his themes are profound. This is like sitting by a fire with a master storyteller whose true power is in the realm of imagination and magic."
—Gabriel Byrne

"Since I was a child, the desolate out islands of the Bahamas have been a home, none more dear than the shark-infested, storm-ravaged, cursed utopia of Rum Cay. . . . *Deep Water Blues* churns with the beauty, desperation, violence, and yearning of those fighting to survive on a speck of land in an eternal sea. As a reader, I am on fire. As a son, I could not be more proud."
—Josh Waitzkin

"Loved this book. I could not put it down. A lifetime of memories of my own fishing these same waters."
—Mark Messier, hockey legend

"*Deep Water Blues* does what all fine literature aspires for—it transports readers to another time and place, in this case, to a sleepy, lush island deep in the Bahamas. Fred Waitzkin writes about life, sex, and violence with aplomb, and Bobby Little is a tragic hero fit for the Greek myths. Hope to see everyone on Rum Cay soon."
—Matt Gallagher, author of *Youngblood*

"*Deep Water Blues* has the ease and compelling charm of a yarn spun late in the evening, the sun gone down and the shadows gathering in."
—Colin Barret, author of *Young Skins*

The Dream Merchant

"Waitzkin offers a singular and haunting morality tale, sophisticated, literary and intelligent. Thoroughly entertaining. Deeply imaginative. Highly recommended." —*Kirkus Reviews*, **starred review**

"Fred Waitzkin took me into a world of risk and violence and salvation that I was loath to relinquish. It's a great novel."

—Sebastian Junger

"*The Dream Merchant* is a masterpiece. A cross between *Death of a Salesman* and *Heart of Darkness*. I believe that in the not-too-distant future we will be referring to Waitzkin's novel as a classic."

—Anita Shreve

Searching for Bobby Fischer

"[A] gem of a book . . . [its] quest is beautifully resolved."
—Christopher Lehmann-Haupt, *The New York Times*

"A vivid, passionate, and disquieting book."
—Martin Amis, *The Times Literary Supplement*

"I've seldom been so captivated by a book." —Tom Stoppard

"Under the spreading chess-nut tree there have been many chess books. To my mind this is the best." —Cleveland Amory

Mortal Games

"Waitzkin captures better than anyone—including Kasparov himself in his own memoir—the various sides of this elusive genius."
—*The Observer*

"Compelling." —*GQ*

The Last Marlin

"A remarkably ambitious and satisfying memoir."
—*The New York Times Book Review*

"When Fred Waitzkin was younger, he thought he had it in him to be a good writer. He was right. This memoir of growing up is passionate, often very funny, very tender, and thoroughly engrossing."
—Peter Jennings

"Finding purity in the rarefied world of big-game fishing was Ernest Hemingway's forte, and he imbued it with transcendent significance. Fred does the same in *The Last Marlin*, but in far more human terms."
—John Clemans, editor, *Motor Boating & Sailing*

"Though there is much sorrow and confusion on these pages there is great beauty—a nearly profligate amount of it—almost everywhere you look . . . clearly one of of a kind and deeply moving."
—*Jewish Exponent*

Strange Love

STRANGE LOVE

A Novel

Fred Waitzkin

Illustrated by Sofia Ruiz

OPEN ROAD
INTEGRATED MEDIA
NEW YORK

Copyright © 2021 by Fred Waitzkin

Illustrations by Sofia Ruiz

ISBN: 978-1-5040-6642-6

Published in 2021 by Open Road Integrated Media, Inc.
180 Maiden Lane
New York, NY 10038
www.openroadmedia.com

for

Bonnie

Katya

Josh

Desi

Jack

Charlie

Antonia

Strange Love

We were seated at a weathered picnic table on the beach behind the Fragata Lounge with a view of old fishing boats tossing on their moorings in the wide bay. The high tide was practically touching our feet. Rachel was across from me talking in Spanish with her aunt, a few cousins, and some others. She had wanted me to meet her family.

Rachel's aunt María José was wearing a tight, low cut dress that left little to the imagination. While María José spoke, Rachel translated in a musical voice trained over the years to rise and fall in counterpoint with the surf. "The women in Fragata are the most beautiful in the world," said María José. She paused to let this sink in. "We're known for this." I guessed she was in her middle fifties, about ten years younger than me.

"Big breasts and butts," she continued. María José was dressed to be noticed and when I took a look, she smiled.

Rachel's aunt had the carriage and confidence of a lady who has been beautiful her entire life. "Men hear about this place and they arrive in luxury convertibles. They have money and after a few days the girls drive off in the fancy cars with hardly a wave. I left when I was seventeen. All the beautiful ones leave."

I looked over at Rachel who had never left, who would like to leave, if someone would take her. Unless that time had already passed for her.

"Really?" I asked while Rachel translated. "Where do they go?"

"They go all over the world," she said, "Spain, New York."

I tried to take this in. Men came to this tiny Costa Rican village of 150 and few more to take away the beautiful women.

"I went to Italy with an older man."

"The most beautiful women in the world?"

"Yes," she said smiling at me. "But when they reach the age of thirty-five or forty, they return here."

The warm Pacific was washing onto my sandals, but the others didn't seem to notice as they ate rice and beans with fried eggs.

Ten days earlier, I'd been driving from the airport along a hot, deeply rutted dirt road to nowhere, or so it seemed. On both sides of the road were rows of skinny teak trees covered by gray dust as if there had been a frost. Occasionally a doleful dark-skinned woman appeared walking slowly toward me from the gloom or a sorrowful cow or several emaciated horses. Every mile or two a little dog appeared to be wandering, confused or sleeping in the road. Then came a six-year-old on a bike pedaling furiously for his life. It was a beaten landscape, which mirrored my state of mind arriving here from New York. Eventually the teak trees gave way to dusty lush mango trees heavy with dangling gray fruit. Sooty air made it challenging to stay on the road as I passed slatted wooden shacks snowed in by road dust with men in undershirts, sitting in chairs, drinking beer, the wash getting filthy on the line. A tiny grocery with its sign obliterated. How did these people breathe?

Until the curtain lifted unexpectedly, gloriously, to the Pacific on the south side of the road, a white beach, trussed on both sides by rocky cliffs, a calm blue-green ocean with a few moored skiffs somewhat protected by a breaking reef fifty yards offshore. A perfect place to cast a line. I stopped for lunch at the tiny fishing village, rickety homes on the beach, several pangas pulled up on the sand beneath palm trees, one huge Guanacaste tree in the center.

Rachel translated as her aunt spoke of the young women taken from Fragata like precious minerals. Meanwhile the others at the table are speaking rapidly in Spanish. I try to grab a word or two. I decide they are saying *I will take Rachel away like all the others.* But does she want that? Or do I?

Unlike her aunt and her younger sister, Sondra, Rachel

never shows her breasts. Even in the heat of the afternoon she dresses modestly in shorts and a loose long-sleeved shirt. At thirty-six Rachel is already too old. It's almost time to come *back* to the tiny village she never left. She feels the sadness of this, and I could love her for it.

A few chickens wander through the sandy yard. Rachel's wash hangs haphazardly across a neighbor's picket fence. Her eighteen-month-old baby, Angelo, is standing in his playpen screaming, let me out.

"How long has this bar been here?" I ask Rachel, who is distracted by her screaming child.

"Why don't you ask my aunt?" she answers curtly. "She came here to speak to you."

I supposed it was true. María José had walked down from a small house on the hill to meet Rachel's new friend from New York. María José and I were a perfect match, an appropriate age difference and she loved good writing. Except the whole story for me was Rachel. I was straining to be polite to her aunt who was dressed for a party.

"How did this place get its start?" I asked.

"My sister, Rachel's mom, bought the property for next to nothing, less than a hundred dollars. Actually, she had a big king-sized bed in her house, sold it and bought the land. She put up a little bar but after a year she lost interest. She wanted to live in San José. She was beautiful then. All the girls here know that their time will pass quickly. They are racing against time."

I was watching Rachel's face while her aunt spoke. When she is relaxed Rachel has a soft welcoming face, but when she is cornered or nervous her face puckers and creases, the coming attraction of old age.

"By luck an older man from the states came here and rented the lounge. That was before we had it fixed up," María José said, a quick trace of smile underscoring her irony. "I met him the year before I left for Italy. We'd talk sometimes on the beach where he liked to sit in the morning to smoke a cigarette. He always carried a book and hummed classical music. He told me about Gabriel García Márquez. He said that this village was right out of a Márquez novel."

As she spoke the tide washed over my ankles. I noticed an old man tossing a handline from a rock a hundred yards down the beach. I wondered what he was fishing for.

"He was a kind man, cultured and gentle. He didn't care for people his own age. He liked children. Each afternoon he invited all the town kids inside the lounge and closed the gate," she continued. "He gave the kids burgers and fries and ice cream. Then he put cartoons on the little TV, and after that, videos with kids touching one another. He was very inventive. He taught the children to play sex games with one another and then he played along with them. These activities went on for several years until he was arrested. One of the little boys from that time, Daniel, still comes here for a beer in the evening. I can introduce you if you like."

7

I nodded yes, but my mind was all over the place. Rachel moved off to the kitchen to prepare the lunch. One of the fishing boats had caught my attention. It was heeled onto its side very close to the building surf. One large wave and the boat would be swamped. María José was looking at me directly, waiting, perhaps for another question. I just wasn't so interested in the history of this run-down place with broken benches and a few torn beach umbrellas.

I smiled to be polite.

"He might tell you more about those days," she said, surprising me with her fluent English. "But he is very moody. Some evenings he is pleasant but other times he sits for hours and won't say a word."

Before leaving, María José told me that she had a home nearby. She pointed to a hill in the distance as an invitation. She had a beautiful smile. From the kitchen, I could smell the shrimps simmering in garlic.

I didn't know what to say to María José. I didn't want to hurt her feelings.

~

It was April, high point of tourist season in Costa Rica. Hotels and restaurants and even broken bars like this one had to make a few colones before torrential rains came in August, and Americans stopped flying into Liberia and San José to party and explore remote beaches. When the rains came the tiny bridges and dirt roads leading to Rachel's village would be flooded out, and the locals would hibernate in damp shabby homes, watch soccer on TV.

Each morning I met Rachel and we sat on torn beach chairs beneath a palm, talking until it was time for her to begin preparing shrimps, red snapper, or chicken on the wood stove, unless Sondra was in a good mood and happened to come in to do the cooking.

"When the pedophile left, the lounge went to shit," Rachel said returning to the story of her life. I had the feeling Rachel had told this story before and would need to tell it again and again. "The way he had it fixed up for the kids was charming, painted in gay colors, animal drawings on the wall. I was studying for one year in San José. I wanted to be a doctor. I'd had this dream from when I was a child. When I came back to visit after he was arrested, drunks and addicts had moved into the lounge. Everything in the place was broken, the stove and refridge were gone. They'd shit and pissed on the floors. The pedophile had made it beautiful. They turned it to sin."

So much of Rachel's passion and remorse went into her story. Occasionally I took her hand while she spoke. It felt like we were together in this beautiful ocean world, joined. But after ten or fifteen minutes, she gently took her hand back.

"It's sweating," she said a little sadly as though it were a malady. She turned over her palm to show me little rivulets of moisture on her palm.

Okay, too hot for holding hands. But just sitting close to her was intoxicating.

"So you came back to the lounge?"

"*Sí* . . . no one else could do it. No more school. I needed to make money for my family. My mom was away with a sea captain boyfriend. Sondra had another life. She's always had another life. . . . I was here. I'm always here. I gave massages to tourists for a year in Nicoya and saved enough to buy a stove and a pizza oven."

Soon we were joined by María José, who often took morning walks on the beach. The two women talked rapidly in

Spanish as if I weren't there. I could hardly catch a word. They would have talked for an hour but I interrupted.

"I was curious about why you said this village is right out of Márquez?"

"Just look around," María José said with her delightful smile. "The beach life is very sexual. Everyone's almost naked."

María José was almost naked in a skimpy bikini. Not Rachel, who was again wearing a long-sleeved white shirt.

"In the North you are super cold and you don't show more than your eyes. The women here are very beautiful, even when they return to the village. A lot of shape. The men are lean and strong from physical work. You're drinking rum at night sitting by the ocean. You're eating seafood. Drink some more. You're almost naked. You're talking with someone, touching a little. You walk down the beach together. It's very natural. . . . Doesn't matter so much who it is, a man or woman . . . or maybe he's the lover of your sister. . . . It's part of the life here."

"Really?"

Rachel nodded, *sí*.

"I need to read Márquez again."

"You don't need to," said Rachel's aunt with her generous smile. "It's all right here."

~

I was thirty years old when I sold my first novel to a renowned editor at Random House, Joe Fox, who had worked on the celebrated fiction of Ralph Ellison, Phillip Roth, and Truman Capote. The day before I went to his office for the first time, Truman Capote's obituary had appeared in the *New York Times* along with quotes from my new editor. On that first meeting, Joe remarked on my "narrative talent," a term I didn't quite understand, and then said to me with his trademark smirk, "I lost Capote yesterday but today I got you." The irony didn't escape me, but I knew the book was good and so did he.

I'd gone from zero straight to the top. Random House, Roth, Capote, and me. While working on revisions for half a year, Fox—that's how he was known in publishing circles—and I became friends. We went drinking together, talked books, sports, and his broken heart after his much younger wife left him. Joe took me to swanky restaurants frequented by literary heavyweights, one night joining George Plimpton and Gay Talese for drinks at Elio's. For sure I was a rookie but we were all on the same team, or so it seemed. I'd made it into the big leagues.

My novel was reviewed warmly by the *New York Times*. My wife showed the review to her girl friends and parents living in Ohio, but in truth, my writer's life and vainglorious aspirations were boring to her. It was a good review but without the superlatives I'd hoped for. In my mind I typed them into the review and over time I came to believe they'd actually been there.

My wife was an Ohio girl who had quickly decided that New York was unfriendly and without redeeming charm. This confused me because New York made me feel alive. Many nights I narrated stories I encountered on the subway or on the street chatting with strangers that occasionally became my characters. I tried hard to win her over, but my fervent shop talk was boring to her. Often when I spoke of my writing, Beth waited a respectful moment or two before flipping on the TV.

Our first months together had been a sexual hurricane, and any differences between us were lost in passion. But over the expanse of seven years, and almost without noticing, we'd become strangers at home. When she finally left me to move back in with her parents, it didn't feel like a catastrophe. In truth, heartache was wonderful to feel again and I coveted what little I had. I could draw on it and put this mistaken marriage into a book.

And I was writing again. That's what I loved, spending days making stories, refining sentences and paragraphs. I wanted to fill a bookshelf with my novels like Roth and Updike. I was certain that I would. Joe was still my friend. The *Times* had referred to me as a "promising young author" and I tried to hold onto that as the years passed.

My second book took me more than five years to complete. Joe wouldn't buy this one, which hurt a lot. His note to me was gentle but brief and I was too insecure to ask for a long explanation. After a dozen rejections my agent sold the book to Putnam. The *Times* didn't review my second novel and those few reviews that appeared in obscure places were south of lukewarm. I tried to rewrite them in my mind so that I could sleep nights.

~

"Maybe you'll write a novel about this place," Rachel said hopefully.

After dinner, we were seated in the lounge on a crude wooden bench across from the bar. The surf had calmed to a pleasant afterthought.

"I'm always looking for a story to write," I said feeling my face flush.

There was romantic Latin music drifting into the lounge from a neighbor's radio. The music, the surf, the smell of the ocean, the smell of her body. It was intoxicating. Rachel was what I wanted. Rachel was my story. I fell for her from the start.

"It's hard to find the right story. The writing is easy if you have a good one. But the right one for you might not be right for me." I reached back for the kind of literary advice I offered twenty-five years earlier when I'd sometimes tutored young authors. But my voice sounded strained. I wondered if she could tell.

"When do you think you'll leave here?" She asked.

Leave?! I couldn't imagine leaving. . . . We hadn't even written the second chapter. There was still so much to decide. I had a little money in the bank. Maybe I could help her run this place. We could fix it up with some new furniture and a paint job. I was stumbling ahead of myself. Why not? With a little advertising, tourists would come from the bigger towns for her delicious seafood. I was swamped with emotion for this woman I hardly knew. Maybe it was the ocean breeze that made me feel a little dizzy.

"I like you so much, Rachel." I was shocked when the words flew out of me. Rachel seemed to be surprised as well. I hadn't intended to. She stopped talking entirely. Almost always Rachel had something to say, but not then. How could she? She didn't know me. I was thirty years her senior. But I'd put it out there for her to look at in the empty lounge and maybe to think about a little later in her sleeping bag on top of the bar.

But after a minute or two I felt alone in a shabby room with a bare light bulb swinging overhead. My words were running past me, promises to a stranger beside me. Did I actually love this unusual woman that I hardly knew? Was it the magic of the place or the despair of a last chance slipping away, or just the nonsense of an old man trying to outrun his considerable failures? We both sat silently on the bench looking around, the muffled sound of the calm ocean, mixing with the sleepy sounds of baby Angelo from his playpen below the bar.

"Excuse me," Rachel said and went to the small soiled bathroom across from the bar.

Or maybe it was just the ocean breeze giving me a shove. I wanted to tell her, *I love you*, right there, that night, in the empty lounge.

And, why not? When I leave here for my lonely room, Rachel will climb onto the concrete bar and sleep on a small, wrinkled sleeping bag that is already in place. Her baby boy will sleep beneath her in his playpen. She doesn't even have money for pampers.

"I'm sorry," she said without explaining why when she sat back beside me on the bench, her hip touching mine. Rachel's manner had turned soft and inviting. When she touched my shoulder with her thin fingers the feeling went through me like an electric charge. But even more, her touch affected me like a promise or a prophesy.

"A few years ago it wasn't like this in the lounge," she said touching me again for emphasis. She wanted me to understand this. "We served pizza. People came for lunch and dinner from nearby villages—some even travelled here from Santa Cruz."

Right then I recalled the words to a song my mom sang to me, when I was a little boy, a haunting Great Depression ballad: "Once I built a railroad, I made it run / Made it race against time / Once I built a railroad, now it's done / Brother, can you spare a dime?"

When I was a writer that song probably informed every story I ever wrote. But that was a long time ago and now Rachel was the storyteller.

"We used to have parties, big parties on the beach with music."

Her English was remarkably good. She seduces with words and unusual juxtapositions. And sadness. She should have been the writer.

High on her inner thigh Rachel has a tattoo of what appears to be the foot of a baby. I yearned to touch it.

"Today, the fishermen here love to touch tiny babies . . . Did María José mention that? They touch them all over."

"What? Their privates? You've seen this?"

Rachel is trying to seduce me with her story.

"Everyone sees. It's natural."

"Natural?"

"*Sí*." She is amused by my surprise.

"The fisherman are the same kids that once came to the lounge?"

"*Sí*."

This lady with knowledge of art and medicine delights in the mores and superstitions of this unusual village even while she plots her escape.

But why not? Rachel has nothing but this empty lounge

open to the sea. Not even money for pampers. It felt like a chance. "Brother can you spare a dime." Thanks Mom, you knew so much.

Lulled by the music of the ocean I had an enormous desire to kiss her. Maybe something more might happen after this. I was high as a kite with hope. It seemed like the right moment with a warm breeze flooding the lounge. I slowly leaned toward Rachel and then she turned her head to the side, offering me her cheek.

~

I never met Joe Fox again for dinner. For months I'd imagined giving him a call. But I could no longer write a decent paragraph. What could I say to Joe? I never made the call. I suppose I'd never been a member of the team, not really.

I was thirty-five and rudderless. None of the girls I dated meant anything to me. I wasn't going to fill a bookshelf like Roth and Updike. What then? For as long as I could remember I was going to be a writer. Until I wasn't anymore.

I visited several old college friends, but they were worn out from children, moving on to homes in the suburbs, stepping from one cobblestone to the next. They asked me if I was working on a new book, although none of them suspected the import of the question. Our talk was deadly. Emptiness does not make for good conversation.

I thought I'd been in the lead. Suddenly I was dead last.

I travelled to a tiny island in the Bahamas that I'd visited several times with my wife, staying in a broken-down hotel with a view of the Atlantic rushing through the outer reef into the harbor. In the afternoons I cast out a line from the dock and caught a few snappers. Often I chatted with an old friend from previous trips, Craig Tenant, who was usually sitting on the gunwale of his weather-beaten boat drinking a Heineken or tinkering with his huge gas engines.

My friend was a genius engine mechanic who loved the challenge of fixing big motors with old spare parts. He was also a lover of writing and a drunk who made money smuggling marijuana from Bimini across the Gulf Stream into Miami. Many afternoons I sat with him on his old 34-foot Pacemaker while he tinkered with his two 650-horsepower gasoline engines torqued up for maximum speed. The name of his boat was *MST*. Built into her shabby interior were compartments that could hold three thousand pounds of grass and hashish. There were frequently shipments of marijuana arriving at the island from Colombia. Every few weeks, when Craig was in the mood, and sober enough to steer *MST* due west to Miami, he carried drugs across the Gulf Stream, and more than once he'd been chased by coast guard speed boats.

Craig and I stayed in touch and he even visited me in New York a couple of times, though he was lost in the city. He'd been a fan of my first book and over the years I'd show him things I was working on. He always laughed in the right spots, noticed ironies and the rhythms of sentences. He got it more than Fox ever had, or at least he made me feel that way.

Craig had this idea that has stayed with me to this day. One drunken evening he told me that after his smuggling days were finished, he wanted to find a little place in the islands, a bar with a small restaurant. He'd call the place, Smuggler's Rest. That's where he would settle and live his last days. The way he drank from dawn he knew there wouldn't be too many last days. He said if I wanted, we could own the place together. It would be a perfect spot for writing or just hanging out, casting a line, and watching the changing tides and sunsets. He was saving his drug money, what was left after drinking, for Smuggler's Rest. I was touched that he asked me to join him there. During my darkest years, I thought about Craig's idea.

I ate dinner each night at Brown's bar, which was mostly empty except for me and a skinny guy who smoked and looked out the window at boats passing in the channel. He had deep cut lines in his narrow hawk face, like my father, chain-smoked and was thin as a rail, like my dad. Except he was a black guy. It took me a couple of dinners before I recognized it was Sammy Davis Jr., grown old. Yes, Sammy Davis from the Rat Pack, Sinatra's best friend. He and I were seated in an empty restaurant, musing in silence, staring at the fast-moving tide or the walls of the dining room adorned with yellowing photographs of large marlin and tuna catches from the past. Sammy Davis looked as sad as I felt.

I'd revered Sammy Davis Jr. since I was a kid. I loved his singing and tap dancing. Once with my wife I'd seen him at Carnegie Hall performing with the great tap dancer Gregory Hines. What a show! Hines was a gorgeous athletic dancer but Sammy was a smoothie, tap danced like Sinatra sang a ballad. On the third night at Brown's I introduced myself. I told him that when I was a kid, I'd seen him on Broadway in *Mr. Wonderful*. Sammy smiled, a saddened version of that lovely smile adored by millions. I told him I was a writer. I had to tell him something; but probably he could tell that I was shot. Strange thing is we were both shot. We both sensed it. We started meeting every night for dinner, talking with great candor like strangers willing to take the risk. He'd just flown here from Vegas where he'd lost almost half a million in a weekend. He told me that time had stopped moving for him. After years of owning the world, he was just walking in place. Something was wrong with his throat, couldn't sing so well anymore. Sammy Davis was staring at the old fishing pictures on the wall telling of past glories on the ocean, trying to figure things out, just like me.

I had a feeling Craig and Sammy would click so I introduced them. I told Sammy how Craig made a living and he seemed curious and amused. One afternoon Sammy walked down to the *MST* and climbed aboard. They got along from the first minute. Sammy crawled after Craig asking questions while they inspected the cramped cabin below with hidden built in compartments where Craig stored the drugs. Sammy was a flyweight, like Craig, same wiry body type, so he was able to work his way between the two 650-horsepower engines tricked out with special carburetors and blowers—the engines were Craig's precious jewels. They were jammed into the small boat with no room to spare. Craig needed to be an acrobat to work on his engines.

"What's *MST* stand for?" Sammy asked.

"Moments of Sheer Terror," Craig answered without a hint of grin.

The three of us sat around the massive engines and Craig explained what it was like to have three coast guard cutters following him across the Gulf Stream. Craig enjoyed teasing the coast guard as they closed in on *MST* that was just ambling west at fifteen knots. And when one of the boats called to him on the loudspeaker to surrender, as Craig knew they would, he slowed *MST* down to a crawl, as if he were going to stop her dead in the water. Then while officers approached in a big inflatable to come aboard to search for drugs, Craig tipped his cap before he threw the throttles all the way ahead and that old Pacemaker came out of the water like an ocean racer. The old boat could sprint across the waves at seventy knots unless the hull broke up or one of his huge beloved engines exploded. Craig lived for these moments of sheer terror—never knowing if he was going to make it to the safehouse in Miami or spend his last years in the penitentiary. Each time Craig jammed his throttles ahead, he knew he'd either shoot away from the pursuing coast guard or he'd blow up. Craig felt most alive in these moments he told Sammy while swigging from the green bottle.

Sammy loved Craig's action, his swag, his legitimacy. Whenever the three of us were together, Sammy mostly talked to Craig. I was a little starstruck by Sammy but Craig was unabashedly himself. By now everyone on the island knew that Sammy Davis was visiting, and while we talked there was always a crowd of fishermen, drunks, and island ladies lingering on the dock at a respectful distance.

From the first, Sammy Davis saw the potential for an action movie. A half dozen afternoons Sammy and I came down to the boat, drank beer with Craig and talked about Moments of Sheer Terror, that's what we'd call it. We told him about Smuggler's Rest and Sammy said, we'd work it into the script. We'd shoot the ending in Smuggler's Rest. He told us he knew the top people at Paramount. We'd need to find the perfect actor for Craig. "Maybe Sinatra," Sammy said. I couldn't believe my ears. Frank Sinatra playing my buddy, Craig Tenant! Sure, I said, recalling how convincing and tragic he'd been in *From Here to Eternity*. The three of us would block out a script and I'd write it. We were on fire with our movie idea.

One afternoon after our movie talk, Sammy climbed off *MST* and couldn't contain himself, did a little tap routine right on the dock beside the old boat just like he'd done with

Gregory Hines in Carnegie Hall. The onlookers applauded and Sammy smiled and tipped his cap.

They were such great days I almost forgot that I was no longer a writer. I knew I could write the hell out of Craig's story. Me and Craig and Sammy Davis Jr.! Craig and I talked about the film a lot after Sammy left Bimini for LA. We would do it for sure. This was our one in a million shot. After that we'd look for the right spot for Smuggler's Rest.

Except Craig ruined the ending. A few weeks after I left the island Craig ran a boatload into Miami and later that night went out drinking to celebrate. In the morning his body was found floating beneath the dock right beside *MST*. Some people said he fell into the canal drunk and drowned but those of us who knew him understood this wasn't possible. Craig was an exceptional swimmer. Almost surely, he'd been murdered by Colombian smugglers who also ran dope to Florida from Bimini and didn't want the competition.

I wrote to Sammy a day or two after hearing about the tragedy and got a one sentence note back from a personal assistant: "Sammy sends his regards." Our friend lived in a very fast lane and he'd already moved on. Months later I was in New York, broke, looking for a job. One night in my apartment channel surfing I ran across a two-hour TV special, a sixtieth-birthday celebration of Sammy Davis Jr.'s life. I watched our friend tap dancing nimble and silky smooth, just as he had on the broken dock beside *MST*.

~

The beach furniture is nothing more than a few boards banged together with rusty bent nails. Each morning before Rachel arrives an old man sits on one of the chairs, staring out to sea; then he starts as if remembering something important, puts out two torn beach umbrellas, although in my weeks there I never saw anyone sit beneath the umbrellas. Yet, each morning the same routine.

Soon Rachel and I settle on two beach chairs I've arranged beneath the palms. The chair digs into my back but I try not to let it show.

A stooped old Tico man walks past us at the water's edge, nods to the other old-timer who is now sitting closer to the bar in the shade. He gives Rachel a toothless smile and she says something I don't understand. It sounds endearing. We watch him slowly hobble to the east end of the beach where he climbs painfully onto the rocks holding a bucket with his bait, a hand-line, and a rudimentary gaff that he uses as a cane. It is a miracle he doesn't fall and gaff himself on the rocks or smash his head.

Rachel looks at her watch and then out to sea probably deciding about today's lunch. I value this hour or two with her each morning before she starts cooking on the wood fire.

"My mom believes in the tarot cards," Rachel says out of the blue, shaking her head in amusement or distaste, hard to say. "Any superstition she believes. She visits a woman, Sylvia, in Nicaragua, whenever she calls, 'You have to come tonight,' Sylvia says

to her. 'We need to talk. I need to read you the cards because something big is coming. You can make money. But I need to work with you. . . .' Some bullshit like this. . . . So, Mom goes to the cash register and takes everything I made in two weeks." She points to a rusting cash register behind the bar. "She takes a shower and gets a lift to San José to fly to Nicaragua to consult with Sylvia. Can you imagine how furious this makes me?"

I nod yes and take Rachel's hand, but my timing is not the best. She's annoyed with Sylvia and pulls her hand free.

"I trying to support my family on the economical part. But it's like a world without an ending. You give her some money and she will give it to this woman with the cards. Oh shit . . . One day, Mom came home from Nicaragua with a little doll head filled with dirt and needles, Sylvia gave to her for me.

Sylvia said, 'Rachel is carrying around bad energy because she doesn't believe.' My mom handed me the doll. 'This will fix it. Keep it with you everywhere you go. But after two weeks you must burn it. Understand? That's important, to burn it.'"

"What did you say to her?"

"I said, 'Yes Mom.' Okay, I burn it after two weeks. . . . I give her the money in the register. I don't argue with her anymore. Then my mom says to me, 'Sylvia told me our family is having bad energy because you don't practice rituals. Evil spirits are trying to get into the family from the back door.' I am the back door. It's my fault, everything that goes wrong in this place."

I notice the old fisherman, Miguel, is at the end of the beach on a flat rock tossing out his handlines. Every morning he is there, throwing his baits past the rocks into the deep water. Maybe to break the monotony of the long afternoon in my room, I'll bring my spinning rod, sit beside Miguel after Rachel goes to work.

"One night my mom was with one of the fishermen," Rachel continues. "They slept in the same bed, but she didn't like him so nothing happened. But the next morning she felt an attraction and they had sex. Just one time, an impulse. She never saw him again but weeks later she realized she is pregnant. She didn't want any more babies but especially not from this guy who is cruel and stupid. She never even told him she got pregnant. She flew to Nicaragua to find out what to do.

Sylvia gave her what to take when she came home. Mom took it but it didn't work. Sondra came out angry and crying. Mom hated her at first. Didn't want to be with her. She didn't want any more babies and especially not this one from that guy. In the first months with Sondra, I was the mom. She cried day and night, drove me nuts.

"Sondra got worse. Nothing would quiet her. She spit out her food. She shit on the floor. Would not use the toilet. She smeared her shit on the walls. Maybe because Mom tried to kill her. I always believed that. Mom was away in Nicoya working. I was the mom. But I wasn't a mom. I wanted to go to school someday and study medicine.

"When she came home to visit, my mother was a changed lady. Maybe it was guilt. I don't know what happened. Suddenly she loved Sondra. It was like night and day. This unhappy little girl meant everything to her. Mom moved back to the village to work in the lounge so she could be with her little girl. She gave her everything. She emptied the cash register. Beautiful clothes. Money to spend on treats. She gave me nothing. For one year I was in school, I was starving and she wouldn't send money. Sondra could do anything she wanted. If I asked her for a few colones it was a war. Sondra didn't need to ask. I was so jealous. Any child would be. Anything she did was okay with my mother. When she was fourteen, she was going to parties with older boys. At fifteen she already had that bod. She was having sex."

Rachel and I are watching a tourist float on his back in the calm water. How did he ever find his way to this remote beach? He's piqued Rachel's interest. Maybe there are others further down the beach. Maybe they heard about the great seafood in the Fragata Lounge and will stop by for lunch. She's so pleased and so am I. Soon she'll cook red snapper in foil on the wood fire. Fresh snapper is delicious cooked this way, and the smell will drift down the beach. Maybe there will be money today in the cash register. I love these morning interludes with Rachel. I feel happy about the tourist floating on his back. I'm looking down the beach for others. I feel like we're making progress.

"When I was twenty-two, I fell in love with an Italian guy," Rachel says to me. "I really loved him. We were two children together playing at life. Giovanni was the man of my heart.

"Days with him were like going to a carnival. His family was very wealthy, although I didn't know at the time. But when I visited him in Italy for two weeks, we drove everywhere in a Mercedes convertible. His parents owned a three-story house right on the beach. He was cultured about music and reading. At the end of my visit he asked me to marry him and I said, of course I would. He was everything a young woman could imagine. I called my mom to tell her the great news. When I returned to Costa Rica, I didn't see him for two months. I yearned for him. Then he travelled here to visit me.

"Every day he dove into the waves, right here." She pointed

at the breaking surf. "He was such a great looking guy. All the girls flirted with him. But none so boldly as my own fifteen-year-old sister who walked with him on the beach, that amazing bod in a ribbon bikini. But so what, she was my sister. It was safe. It even made me proud that she liked him. Until one night they drank rum together and then walked down the beach. When they came back to the lounge they were holding hands. I was so embarrassed. What could I say to them? I couldn't look at him. My fifteen-year-old sister was fucking him. I wanted to kill them, or kill myself.

"Mom and I were serving dinner, when they came by holding hands. 'Finally she's got a good one,' my mother said to me. 'That's the kind of guy I want my son to be. I don't know why you let him escape, Rachel.'

"I wanted to run away but to where? There was no place for me but here. I needed to take care of the lounge. Every piece of food we ate came from the lounge. I needed to feed the customers and smile while she fucked my boyfriend. That was my job. Is still my job."

$\sim$

One morning I came into the lounge and Rachel wasn't there. The shuttered place was damp and empty and smelled of old beer. I sat at the bar for ten or fifteen minutes, wondering where she was and then used the bathroom. The tiny soiled

room smelled awful and there was no toilet paper. Rachel's toothbrush was resting in a cup. I went back to the bar. It didn't seem like the same tropical dream without her.

When I was about to leave for my room, Rachel's thirty-year-old sister walked into the lounge. Sondra said a few words in Spanish I didn't understand. "*Mas despacio, por favor,*" I asked, please slow down. She repeated in broken English that her sister was off with Angelo to a doctor in another village.

At first look Sondra appeared to be completely nude. In fact, she was wearing a narrow band of material on top that covered only a small cross section of her large breasts and only part of her nipples. Below she wore a thong, but her ample size swallowed up these pieces of material and gave the impression she was wearing nothing at all. I realized I was staring and when I averted my eyes, Sondra was amused.

She told me that she had come this morning to cook lunch.

"Are you hungry?" she asked though it wasn't close to lunch time.

I stumbled for an answer. Sondra had this effect on me, as if there were a dialogue running beneath the dialogue. She knew that I came to the lounge mornings to visit her sister and this seemed to spark some interest. But why should she be interested in me? I had no money to speak of. I was old. These thoughts afflicted me from the moment she pulled up a high stool beside mine.

"Rachel and I usually meet here in the morning," I said just to say something.

"I know," she answered. When Sondra turned to talk to me her naked breast brushed my left arm. I couldn't tell if this was unnoticed or if she was playing with me.

"I think my sister have depression about her life," Sondra reflected in broken English. "She should think before she had a baby with no father. She never think about nothin'. I think she have a little depression."

I was sweating in the mid-morning heat. She asked if I wanted a soda. With each question or remark her breast lingered on my arm and shoulder. Her smile and the warmth and size of her naked body had a powerful effect.

"Maybe my sister can't find the right man. Always looking for the perfect man."

"It's hard to find the right person."

Sondra had an inviting smile. And I could smell each breath. I flashed on a scene from a Fellini film that has stayed with me. A middle-aged man becomes infatuated with a gorgeous larger than life actress, Anita Ekberg. But when he meets her in the flesh, she is as large as her image on a billboard. He wants to feel her breasts, to kiss them but they are so large that they nearly suffocate him. She tempts him and laughs in his face.

"Rachel not be back for an hour," she said, looking me over.

I imagined her laughing at me while I slinked away

ashamed, not knowing what to do with her sheer size and the urgency of my temptation.

"The right man, it's a lot of sugar." She laughed at her metaphor. "It's hard to find him. Maybe you find the right man for six months and move on. You come to this life alone. Maybe nobody's forever. You undersan?"

I nodded yes.

What a pair. One sister tells everything but covers her body. The other only speaks in riddles and cooks in the nude.

Was our moment an invitation or a muted threat? I couldn't tell. I don't know. I couldn't read Sondra, who soon moved to the little kitchen at the end of the bar, put on a little green apron over her thong and began simmering shrimps in garlic.

~

Another morning, María José pulled up a chair and joined us on the beach. Rachel took my hand while her aunt sat beside us and breathed in the gorgeous morning. Perhaps she wanted her aunt to see she was desired by a famous writer from the States. María José looks after Rachel, tries to allay her bitterness.

Many women in this part of the world become wrinkled by the sun or else become fat, but María José remained as beautiful and stately as an Italian countess. She had spent formative years of her life in Europe and though she had little formal schooling she'd learned the world reading the novels of Italo Calvino, Tommaso Landolfi, and her favorite, Gabriel García Márquez. She was an open-minded adventurous soul who now savored life's wildness from her porch on the mountain overlooking the Pacific.

Over time it had become clear that locals were close-mouthed about the mores of their world, perhaps fearing loose talk might invite problems from the outside world. Sondra, free lover though she was, walked from us in disgust one morning while Rachel and her aunt talked to me about the unusual sexual predilections in the village. Turning back, she'd said acidly, "I know nothing of this."

"Enrique lived in Paris and New York," María José recalled. "He came here about forty years ago, long before the pedophile that rented the lounge. He dressed in fancy clothes like a model and had a lot of money. He came to relax, to have fun. He came with a boyfriend and they bought a small piece of land on the beach." She pointed in the direction of the rocks from which Miguel tossed his handline. "He was a chill guy, very intelligent. He liked me. He told me stories about New York and Paris. It gave me an appetite to see these places. He enjoyed beautiful girls, but he only went with guys.

"After his boyfriend returned to Paris, Enrique went with handsome young men who did what he asked for money. Soon local fishermen began to experiment. They drank rum in the evening and then walked down the beach to play with younger men. No one would have imagined such a thing happening in Fragata because this is a very machismo place. The fishermen didn't think of it as being gay or queer. To have young male lovers became a test of masculinity. And these habits soon became natural like the tides and the rain in August. Fishermen had their wives and their boyfriends.

"Normal is different is here," María José continued. "In the afternoon on the beach fifteen-year-olds grab each other's privates. In the fields they line up to enjoy sex with female horses. They make jokes about it. *Pega yegua.*

"*Sí, pega yegua,*" Rachel echoed her aunt.

María José and Rachel were both amused to surprise a sophisticated New Yorker.

"No one cares," said María José. "When they get a little older the men make babies with two or three sisters from the same family, the ones that didn't leave the town. Maybe there's no normal in Fragata. It is just the life."

"This is still true today, María José? About the fishermen and the young men?"

"In the lounge they write notes to their lovers," she answered, with a shrug. "I have some money for you. I will see you tonight on the beach."

María José was Rachel's elixir, trapped in the lounge, but readily falling into the embrace of her aunt's worldly vision. If only she had been able to escape this place for a while like her aunt. Maybe she still could.

"All the fishermen?" I asked.

"*Sí*," they both answered.

"Do their wives know?" They shook their heads to say, what did it matter.

"What about Miguel?" I asked pointing down the beach.

"*Sí*. Long ago he had a young boyfriend, but he died of AIDS. Now Miguel lives quietly with his wife."

~

The Fragata Lounge is imperiled and heightened like a dare. Will it survive the next storm? On windy days, the waves power across the reef, battering the fleet of old fishing boats, washing over the sand and creeping into the lounge, nearly reaching the bar where Rachel sleeps above her baby. One rogue wave and the whole village will disappear, the boats and broken beach furniture, the lounge itself with its sordid passionate history, no more party nights with delicious red snappers grilling on the wood stove, all gone, a village of gay fishermen with their wives and young lovers, broken wooden shacks with SKY TV dishes and tender molested babies, all of it washed into the sea, with María José watching from the hills. One wave. It's coming for sure, but not yet, please. I've just met Rachel.

It's Rachel's habit to make me wait for twenty minutes or longer on the beach chair by the water until she comes out of her shower or from the kitchen where she does her wash in the sink where she cleans fish, carries a few pitiful wet things in her arms and tosses them haphazardly on her neighbor's picket fence to dry.

"When I was eighteen, I didn't look like a girl, no boobs. No boyfriends." Rachel recalled. "Sondra had many boyfriends and she was just a kid. People noticed her more. But I didn't care, because I was smart. She was smart too, but she never used her head for anything.

"Two months after Giovanni left for Italy my sister got pregnant from another boy. Three fifteen-year-old girlfriends decided to get pregnant at the same time. They all had babies the same month, like a game. Can you believe? They had pregnancy celebration. As soon as Sondra started to get a belly, she decided she didn't want it. She wanted to go to parties. My sister hadn't yet learned about remorse.

"She went to our aunt, not María José, another aunt who said to my sister, 'Don't worry. I will go to the drug store, get medicine. Drink it and everything will be okay.'

"I screamed at my aunt. 'How can you say such a thing to her? She is just a child herself. She doesn't know anything. You want to kill her?'

"I pleaded with my sister. 'Don't listen to her. You are too far along. The medicine could kill you.'

"'I will take the baby,' I said to Sondra. 'You can treat her like your little sister. I will take care of you both.'"

Rachel looked at me as if sizing up how this moment might work in the novel I will write.

"You always pick up the broken pieces in your family," I said to her. "You're so sensible."

Rachel leaned over and kissed me gently on the lips, the softest kiss you can imagine. I was amazed, thrilled. This beach morning was a kind of celebration, the ocean nearly still, a few birds circling above a school of small bar jacks splashing in the shallow water a dozen feet from us. I thought about shouting to Miguel on the rocks, "Over here, the fish are right here," but Miguel wouldn't have cared. He was into his own music. Later that morning Rachel had tossed her beautiful naked leg over mine and after a minute or two I touched the tattoo of her nephew's foot on Rachel's soft inner thigh and she didn't mind. When I got hard, I wondered if she'd say something, but she didn't seem to notice.

"So what happened?" I asked Rachel.

"I was serving lunch in the lounge, a big group sent from one of the hotels in Tamarindo. I was running from table to table carrying trays of food and taking orders when she called my cell. My sister was crying, I could hardly hear the words, customers shouting for beer and more shrimps. 'I think I'm gonna give birth now and I'm alone. I'm really scared.'

"Of course she's scared. She's only fifteen. Everyone wants food, mixed drinks, and I'm trying to smile at the customers and talk on the phone.

"'Where's Mom?' I asked her. Sondra started weeping and could barely get out the words. 'She left for Nicaragua.'

"'For what?' Sondra didn't answer. My mother wasn't at the hospital. She didn't tell me she was leaving Sondra. I hung up, told the guy who cooks the pizza to collect the money, when the phone rang again. Sondra, she was now laughing hysterically. Oh my god, she's such an asshole. 'Sondra, what's wrong with you?'

"'I don't know. I just feel bad.' She couldn't stop laughing.

"I ran out of the lounge, got a friend to take me to San José on his motorcycle. When I got to the hospital my sister was having seizures. She couldn't breathe. When they got her into surgery, she had a heart attack. She was dying and the baby was dying also. What the fuck was my mother doing with Sylvia? She didn't even call us. She should have been with her daughter. A doctor came out of surgery and said, 'Your sister is really bad. She might not make it. We need your consent. If we have to decide, do you want to save the baby or your sister? You have to tell me right now!'

"My fucking mother. This wasn't for me to decide. I was a kid myself. I said, 'Save Sondra.'"

~

I started spending three or four afternoons a week on the rocks down the beach from the lounge, seated next to Miguel, casting out a lure with my spinning rod. We'd nod hello in the morning and then hardly talk while we fished. I caught a few small snappers and tossed them back. I really didn't care so much about catching fish, but it was lovely sitting close enough to the reef to feel the salt spray and to fall into the rhythm of casting the lure. I'd learned from Rachael that Miguel had torn up his right shoulder many years earlier fighting a large fish. Now he tossed his line out using his left hand. I had the feeling the old man had long ago caught enough for three lifetimes and didn't care anymore about killing fish. These afternoons were his last song.

Miguel had once been the best fisherman in this village of fishermen, Rachel told me. All the local men fished two in a boat, a mile or two off the beach, for red snapper, grouper, and when they were running, small dorado. Miguel always fished by himself, but when he came back to the beach at sunset he always brought in the biggest catch. For a long while the other fishermen were jealous and tried to see what secret baits he was carrying out in the morning; but eventually they came to accept the truth that his instinct for the ocean and the habits of fish was on a higher level. They no longer felt jealous. He was the king of their realm.

After years outfishing every other skiff in the village, Miguel had become bored with the daily routine of inshore snapper fishing, Rachel had told me. One morning at dawn, while the others were still asleep, he brought an extra tank of fuel, steered his small skiff way offshore and dropped his handlines deep into the ocean like Cuban fishermen many years ago. It was dangerous to go so far in a wooden skiff with a small outboard. If the weather turned bad or if his small engine failed there was no one to find him drifting in the Pacific. Occasionally other fishermen had considered offshore trips but snapper fishing close to the village was so good that no one was willing to take the risk, except Miguel. Fishing for two- and three-pound snappers no longer engaged his imagination. He quickly discovered the different secrets of deep-water fishing. He learned to fish the rips and weed lines for big wahoo and dorado. If he saw a school of spinner dolphin leaping in the distance, he steered his boat close by so that he could troll lines for hefty yellowfin tuna that swam beneath the dolphin.

Some evenings Miguel came back to the beach with his sixteen-foot skiff loaded down with five or six fat eighty-pound tuna, enough to feed the entire village. Some days his boat was loaded with fifty- and sixty-pound dorado. Locals always waited on the beach to see what miracle catches Miguel would toss onshore right in front of the lounge. The other men were tempted to go offshore to compete but they were afraid. No one here had navigational equipment to find their way home. Miguel navigated by instinct. He never worried about finding his way back. He sensed the direction of the tiny harbor and steered his skiff back to the winding river through the reef into the harbor in front of the Fragata Lounge.

One evening Miguel didn't return to the beach. All the fisherman became concerned. When he wasn't back after dark a few of the men lit a big driftwood fire on the beach in front of the lounge and tended it through the night so he could get a bearing from way offshore. But he didn't return. The following morning men and women stood on shore searching for a glimpse of his boat. Nothing. Bad luck had finally caught up with Miguel, the men speculated. He'd ventured too far offshore in a small boat.

Late in the afternoon two old men on the beach saw a

smudge on the horizon. When the skiff drew closer and began to navigate the winding channel that cut through the reef, they could see there was a huge fish lashed alongside. Miguel steered to shore with a fourteen-foot black marlin lashed to the side of his skiff, just like Hemingway's old man, Santiago. There was no scale in the town so it's hard to say how big it was, perhaps six or seven hundred pounds, surely smaller than Santiago's giant marlin, but still much, much larger than any fish anyone had ever seen in the village.

Miguel's hands were badly cut and bleeding from a sixteen-hour fight on his handline. By the time he reached the outer reef and the little channel into the tiny harbor he realized he'd made a terrible mistake. Miguel had read Hemingway's book in Spanish when he was a boy. It was something he had wanted to try to do himself. That was fifty years ago. But now with the big marlin lashed alongside, and many friends pointing at his skiff heeled over from the weight of the marlin, he fully appreciated the emptiness of the gesture. Local people wouldn't eat the coarse meat of a marlin unless there was a famine. The waters just offshore of the village were replete with delicious dorado and red snapper and the big female black marlin was tough as leather. It was a terrible waste to kill such a fish. The old man idled in with the marlin and pushed his bow onto the sand in front of the lounge. All the fisherman looked on in awe. They'd never seen such a fish, but after an hour they all went back to their homes. Miguel put the outboard on his shoulder and walked slowly to his shack, never turning back to look at the giant marlin lashed to his skiff.

The following morning when he returned to the skiff some small reef sharks and jacks were ripping up the bottom half of the great fish that was still hanging in the surf. What a waste. He'd killed the marlin for empty glory. This singularly great catch essentially ended the fishing life for Miguel who was already in his late fifties. He went out a few more times in the skiff for snappers but the fishing didn't excite him, and he soon stopped going. On a full moon high tide, Miguel pulled his skiff up the sand behind his shack on the beach and after four or five years the bottom rotted out from rain and the beating sun. Some of the planks and cross members are still there today, like the bones of a large animal.

Fishing from the rocks, Miguel no longer rates the success of an afternoon by the numbers or size of his catch. He is fishing for other things. He throws out his line while I cast my own. Occasionally when one of us catches a small snapper we toss it back in.

Most of the village fisherman weren't born or were just kids when Miguel made his great catches trolling and deep dropping twenty miles out in the Pacific. Some of the old-timers recall the tremendous marlin he dragged in through the reef but for most in the village that was a myth and Miguel was just the old man who tosses a handline from the rocks at the end of the beach.

In the late afternoon Miguel and I lean against two old wooden poles that had been driven into the rocks years before, probably part of the supports for a beacon to help the fish boats find their way back in the evening. I usually bring a couple of beers in a small cooler and we drink the beers looking out at the water. Mostly we don't talk, but once I asked him if he ever thought about the huge tuna and dorado he'd brought in to the village many years ago . . . if he could still do it today. "*¿Todavía hoy?*" He looked at me as if I was stupid. "*Seguro hombre*," he answered.

I usually stay on the rocks until sunset when I go back to my room and take a shower before going to the lounge for fresh snapper or Rachel's shrimps with garlic, rice and beans, and plantains, which is my favorite. Often, I am the only one in the lounge eating, but occasionally another couple is dining, having driven from one of the tourist towns, Nicoya or Tamarindo.

~

I loved nights with Rachel after food and a few glasses of wine, the moist sea air rushing through the lounge like a wind tunnel. We held hands on the wide bench with both of her beautiful long legs draped over mine, while she told me her story with urgency until her hand became sweaty and began to distract her. She'd shake her hand and before drying it on her shorts she'd show me the moisture on her palm. "See what happens?" I even loved that and nodded sympathetically. She was so wacky and soulful. There was music in Rachel's voice along with suffering and poverty that touched me deeply. I tried not to think too much about where I fit in.

"After Silvano was born my mom didn't like him at all. 'I don't want to see him.' She said 'I don't want to touch him. He almost kill my daughter.' I said to her, 'Mom, what the hell are you talking about? He's your grandson. You left Sondra to go to Nicaragua. I can't believe you did that. What's wrong with you?'"

"Did she feel remorse?"

"She attacked me. She always attacks me. 'You're the problem, Rachel. Sylvia wants me to bring you so she can read the cards. She told me you in the circle of death, someone's gonna rape you and cut you to pieces. And I will never know what happened to my daughter. She wants to see you Rachel!'

"Oh my god, you have no idea. It's been like this my entire life. Half the time Mom gets angry with me and I have no idea why. Because she has a premonition. 'Shut up Mom. Don't even talk to me.'"

Sometimes I get giddy with Rachel's story and try to give her a kiss, but usually she shakes me off—don't you know this isn't the moment? She's busy telling the story of her life that I will write to make her a famous lady one day.

"Sondra was a party girl, and still is. She didn't want to take care of her baby. She wanted to go to parties, parties, parties. Always a new boyfriend. 'I'm your fun number one', she told each one of them." Rachel giggled at the absurdity. 'I'm your fun number one.' Imagine saying that?"

Yes, but I sensed Rachel envied her sister for her excesses and absurdity. Maybe Rachel would have liked to have been some boy's fun number one.

"Sondra was even more gorgeous after her baby. She wanted to dance. She loved to dance. Okay, my mom always agreed with her, she should go out and I would look after Silvano. For some reason that was my job. Whenever I wasn't working in the lounge I should watch Silvano. Whenever I wanted to go out Mom was always pissed. Whenever I argued with her, she would answer, 'No, your sister needs to go out. Don't you care about your sister?'

"Sondra's three-year-old little boy had unusual wisdom but he learned about sadness way too early. After dinner Mommy was always dressing up for the party. She liked to go to a bar with music that was just down the road. 'Momma, don't go,' Silvano would plead with her. 'I want you to stay with me. I want you to sleep with me.'

"'No, no,' she said to her baby. 'I'm going. But I'll come back soon. I'll come back in ten minutes.' Silvano knew where his mommy was going. He'd walk to the door and call down the road after her. Half the village heard him calling, 'Mommy come home. Come home. I want to sleep. I can't sleep without you.' It broke his heart. He stood in the doorway and called and called to her. She turned and waved to him but wouldn't come back."

When the night grew late Rachel bent her head toward mine and gave me kisses on the mouth, her lips moving a little the most beautiful kisses you could imagine, filled with meaning and amazement. I always wanted more of them, but she always knew when it was enough. Then Rachel went into a small purse and took out a lip gloss, covered her lips and looked into her mirror. That was the signal that our night was finished. If I tried to kiss her once more she shook her head, no. That was it. Rachel knew where to draw the line. Until one night she threw her arms around my neck and offered more kisses. I loved the taste of her lip gloss, and then her tongue exploring my lips and slowly entering my mouth. We kissed deeply while I felt her small breasts and belly, which was still a little big from Angelo (I loved that) and she giggled when I kissed under her arms. I whispered that I'd brought a condom. Rachel shook her head, no, "I don't like." But I really didn't care. I was even a little relieved because maybe I'd forgotten how. She and I sat on the bench holding hands surrounded by the crash and tangy smell of the ocean.

~

After Craig's death I couldn't find the old charm in any of my favorite Village restaurants. I couldn't find life in the underlined paragraphs in my favorite books by Hemingway and Márquez. By then my old college friends, the several that had remained in Manhattan, were deep into the middle game of careers and families. Once or twice over beers I tried to summon the sweet dream of Smuggler's Rest. Craig's idea still felt like a beautiful living thing, but my college buddies patronized me as if I were a lunatic.

One evening walking in Midtown I came across George Plimpton who was speaking with another man in front of a steak restaurant on Fortieth Street. I was so happy to run into him as if we were once intimate friends. George had a charming smile that entreated you to smile back. I walked up to him and threw out my hand expecting a warm greeting. But Plimpton seemed surprised or perhaps annoyed. I reminded him of our evening six or seven years earlier at Elio's with Gay Talese and Joe Fox, and all but said aloud, of course you remember, George! It had been a wonderful night of comradery and book talk. Plimpton shrugged, and said a few cursory words, and then continued his conversation with the other man. For that brief moment I'd forgotten I was no longer on the team. I walked home down Sixth Avenue finding refuge in Mom's favorite depression song. "Once I built a railroad, now it's gone. Buddy can you spare a dime."

After I gave up my Village apartment, several friends

offered me vacation homes to live in until I got back on my feet. I lived in the woods and then on a winter lake and then on the Jersey shore and then again in the woods and on the lake. I took long walks and tried to imagine what to do now that I would no longer fill a bookshelf. I reached out to four or five magazines that had reviewed my first novel inquiring about freelance work. I got one discouraging reply from an editorial assistant.

For three years I came into the city once a week and taught literature classes to seniors at the YMCA on Fourteenth street. My students were between the ages of seventy-five and ninety. One year my theme was mutability in modern literature focusing on *Death in Venice* and the short fiction of Thomas Mann. My course was very popular, perhaps in part because the subject of death was something they all wrestled with. I became very attached to my students and whenever one of them missed a couple of classes there was tension, and questions were asked about what had happened to him or her. This intensity filtered into our discussions of *Death in Venice*, and frankly speaking, made the story itself even more gripping. Three of my students passed away that spring semester.

I was almost dead broke and missing my life in the city when I came across an ad in the *Village Voice* for pest control operators. I wasn't exactly sure what that was. I stopped by the company's office on Twenty-Eighth Street and had a nice conversation with Andy, the owner of the business. The job paid ten bucks an hour. It seemed to amuse Andy to hire a published novelist to work as one of his exterminators.

Andy's company had a large office with six or seven good-looking women hectically scheduling appointments for exterminators, setting up appointments for recruits like me, fielding complaints from angry customers overrun with vermin. Hefty sullen men were entering the office to stuff supplies into their rolling bags. Each day men were quitting because they couldn't handle the work anymore and Andy or one of the women was recruiting new ones. On first take the bedlam of the office reminded me of a section of Henry Miller's *Tropic of Capricorn*, where young Henry takes a job as a recruiter at an insanely busy messenger service and revels in addressing unhappy staff turnover along with the sexual opportunity of innumerable women begging for jobs. Andy's business was really quite different.

One of the guys showed me a few things in the office and the next morning they sent me out with a large rolling bag filled with different kinds of poisons, traps, pesticides, sprays, gloves, knee pads, hammers, scissors, and a few other things. I'd been without a regular job for a long time. I told a girl I was dating that I'd do just about anything for ten dollars an hour. I told her I'd do this work for a while and then find something better. But meanwhile we'd be able to go out for sushi.

My first appointment was in an old diner on the Lower

East Side. At 4 a.m. I went into the place wearing my full body exterminator uniform with a surgical mask, goggles, and a pink headband. As I'd been directed, I crawled under a greasy oven to search for roaches and mice. I found a couple of silver box traps loaded with live mice. I felt good about this for my first time out, like managing to catch fish when you didn't know what you were doing. I crawled out covered in rancid grease holding a box of live mice in each hand.

No one told me what to do with live mice, so I flushed them. It spooked me but it felt like the right thing so I forced myself to look. I watched two of them swimming around the bowl. One of the mice struggled hard, swam as hard as he could, survived flush after flush after flush. He wouldn't go down. The other one struggled for a while. But then, he gave up and went down without much of a fight, as if he were accepting death.

I held the survivor under water with my gloved hand.

As the new guy on the job, the more experienced exterminators would make me do menial stuff, jump down the elevator pit to fight water bugs and rats, but I didn't care. I actually liked it.

I played it like a voyeur, taking notes in my head like Tim O'Brien fighting in Vietnam or George Plimpton practicing for a week with a professional hockey team, except Plimpton would never have crawled under greasy stoves and into rat infested basements. He was a mandarin and this work was disgusting. But it was also hilarious. I could imagine writing about this—if I were still writing—and it was amusing to talk about at night with old friends over beers. For some reason extermination work didn't seem as off-putting to them as Smuggler's Rest. Maybe because it was more plausible, as if I'd finally grown up and gotten serious about my life.

For me this work was another brief stop along the road. I played all sorts of mind games with myself while the months and years flew by.

~

Rachel thought that I was some big shot writer—that opened the door for us. I wasn't courting her to write a novel but that's what she thought and wanted. Maybe it would have been better if I'd told her my history killing vermin. It might have appealed to her raunchy humor, but I didn't and it seemed too late for revising my story.

It didn't bother me that there was inequity in our affection. Maybe this was a function of my age or my stretch of years working in filthy basements and elevator shafts. But I don't think so. When I was a writer, I always found love relationships with unequal measures of attraction and commitment the most interesting. If ours was a kind of business deal in the making, it was fine for me. We both had things to give. If I could help her and make her happy and hold her, listen to her stories, that seemed like a lot for a lonely guy. Most nights we kissed, we touched. It was beautiful and I didn't ask for more. The unlikely nature of all of this working into a long lovely future and the lie at the center of my courting, these issues disappeared during our amorous late nights.

"What we have is much more beautiful than fucking," she said to me one late night. "It's more like the feeling of love." That moved the hell out of me.

~

Some days in front of the lounge the ocean is quiet and calm but disarming as a prophesy. Some days it is friendly. But every day, stormy or quiet, the old man casts his lines from the rocks. Like a sentinel. He nods to Rachel and me each morning as he carries his gear to the rocks where I'll join him after lunch. Rachel and I sit in our beach chairs, holding hands. Yes, it's moved on to that. When she's in the mood she kisses me and runs her hand through my hair.

When I sit with her listening to the story, I'm more like the younger man who wrote two novels. I ask her leading questions. I am amused by her ironies. Her kisses pull me back there to him. She has laid herself open to him. I haven't been that man for nearly thirty years.

After a moment taking in the beauty of the morning, Rachel

continues along the crooked path of her story. "My sister left this village at eighteen like other beautiful girls here, although she wasn't swept away by an aging prince driving a Mercedes. She was sick of motherhood, the little she did. Sondra travelled to Long Island where other poor girls from Costa Rica and Colombia were hired in the summer to harvest marijuana. It was brutal work, fourteen hours a day, bending, cutting, gathering—not right for my sister. After a week or two she was in bed with the owner of the farm and doing a little office work, dancing in the clubs at night. She stayed with him for six months until she grew bored and met an older man, an architect with a place in East Hampton and a fancy apartment in the city.

"So I became the mom of my sister's little boy," Rachel said. "Actually, Silvano was like a little man. He'd lie next to me in the morning, leaning on his elbow with his nose almost touching mine, watching me wake up still exhausted from putting the lounge back together in the night, '*¿Te sientes bien, Rachel?*' Then he'd give me a hug and kiss. 'Take a rest, Rachel.' He could tell whenever I was tired or lonely or sad. He was a little child and already watching out for me—he's the only one in my family who did. I swear he could read my mind. He'd bring me hand cream before I left for work or a mango or a piece of candy. Just what I was craving.

"Some mornings a teenage girl came to watch Silvano when it was time for me to get back to the lounge. But he begged me to take him and made a fuss when I wouldn't. At five years old he swept the floor or hung the wash out back while I prepared the food for lunch. At night I hugged him in bed when I was back from work and he always woke to give me a kiss. Sometimes in the early morning I'd reach to give him a hug and his body felt all stiff, like there was wood in his arms and legs. He'd cry a little. 'What's hurting baby?' That scared me, but Silvano said, '*Esta bien, Rachel. No te preocupes.*'

"Sondra was living the high life in the city. Eating in fancy places with her man. Going to clubs mostly by herself because her boyfriend liked to stay home and read. I was taking care of the business, taking care of Silvano. My mom was mostly away with her sea captain boyfriend. I never knew where she was. We were doing good in the lounge. We were making pizza. I had a terrific guy who could make it good as in New York. There was money. I had a new motorcycle. Those were the best of times."

I think it was that morning, but it may have been another. I stood up to stretch my back from the beach chair, and when I turned around, I saw Sondra, standing behind us in the shadow of the lounge. She was dressed in her bikini, hands on her hips as though she were making a judgment. I don't think she was close enough to hear us, but I wasn't sure.

I turned back to Rachel and whispered something about it, and she turned around to look.

"No, she's not there now."

But after this I felt her sister was always around, lurking. She was a presence, inside and outside Rachel's story.

Rachel was finished for the morning, and thinking about something else, maybe what to cook on the wood fire. It was almost time to go to work. "Rachel, you were a kid when you loved Giovanni. Was there anyone after him . . . that you really loved?"

She hesitated for a moment, shook her head no, but then seemed to reconsider. "One time," she said standing up from the beach chair, "There was a guy visiting from Spain. He had a big motorcycle and he'd drive slowly through the village. He was beautiful, black hair, a great bod. I talked to him a few times when he stopped the motorcycle outside the lounge. I knew if this guy touched me I'd fall for him. I'd go anywhere

he asked. I'd do anything he wanted. I knew it and I think he knew. He made me float in the air."

She stopped talking.

"That was it?"

"There was a little more. He was a surfer and every morning he dove into the waves for a swim before he went out with his board. One day I decided to follow him. It was a wonderful morning, the ocean glistening. My bod was more beautiful then," Rachel said touching her breasts. "That morning I looked at myself in the mirror. I was the most beautiful in my life, right then. Maybe because of this guy. I put on the tiniest bikini and followed him into the sea. We swam together and said a few things. Nothing much. When we came out of the water we kissed . . . That was it."

"Why, that was it? Why didn't you see him again? He sounds great."

"I was already eight weeks pregnant with Angelo. I was living with a guy."

~

Late on a hot stuffy night in the lounge: "Out of the blue, Sondra called from New York and said she was coming home," Rachel recalled bitterly. "Two days later she was back in Fragata. She had her adventure like all the other young women and after nearly four years it was time to return. She missed home. Her architect boyfriend was crazy about her, but she was bored staying home nights with him. That's what she said, but probably he kicked her out for fucking around. A few days later Mom was back from travels with her seaman. They were both back. Mom wanted to hear about Sondra's New York life, the discos and restaurants. They were inseparable. Mom never asked two questions about the lounge, which had been doing great. You'd think they'd be curious. I'd been sending money to her and my sister each month. Sondra was back with that smile and bigger-than-life figure. She missed the beach life, the sun, the beautiful young men.

"Soon after she got back, I invited her to come with me to a costume party in a private house. I dressed up like the black widow. I don't know, maybe I looked beautiful or dangerous. Guys wanted to flirt with me. A couple of guys asked me out for drinks after. This kind of thing didn't happen very often. Flirtations for me were mainly in the lounge serving booze with some drunk saying, 'You wanna fuck?' Sondra had been sitting by herself watching. I'm not a vain person— I think you know that. But it made me feel good in front of my beautiful sister.

"Couple of days later she came to me and said it was time for her to move back in with her kid—he was eight now and needed to have a mommy. Needed to have a mommy!

"She raved about Silvano to our mother. Sondra bragged about his intelligence and caring. She described his sensitivity and called him a little man. That's what I had told her. She went on and on about him as if she'd written the book, and Mom ate it up. After four years, I had been dismissed. Sondra moved into the room in María José's house with Silvano. I was out, back in the lounge, sleeping on the bar."

Rachel pointed to her sleeping bag on top of the bar. She'd been mostly living here for the last seven years. I hugged her and tried to give her a kiss, but she turned away toward the filthy green wall. She averted her face for a long time. She wouldn't say a word. When Rachel turned back to me, tears were rolling down her cheeks and onto her white blouse, but she never made a sound. Her cheeks and blouse were drenched. I've never seen anyone cry like that. I wanted to hold her, but she wouldn't let me.

~

The following morning when I walked through the front door of the lounge, I saw ten or twelve men surrounding Miguel who was seated on one of the beach chairs. Rachel was seated beside him on the other chair and for some reason the old man was showing the bottoms of his feet. When I drew closer I saw his hands were cut up and I guessed he'd fallen off the rocks. The other men were throwing questions on top of one another and slapping Miguel on the back. The old man calmly told his story in rapid Spanish, much of which I couldn't understand.

Both of his hands were bleeding, but he didn't seem to care. After the better part of an hour the crowd broke up, and Miguel slowly hobbled back to his little shack. Here is what Rachel told me.

Yesterday evening, there had been a cool breeze coming off the ocean under a full moon. It seemed a shame to go back to his cramped stuffy place, and anyhow Miguel's legs were hurting, and he wasn't looking forward to climbing down the rocks and limping down the beach. But also he felt something happening, a kind of premonition some fishermen have. Miguel hadn't felt this in a long while.

It was the start of an outgoing tide and small fish were breaking on the surface in the deep water past the reef. All afternoon he'd been catching two-pound snappers and tossing them back. "Why not try?" he said to himself. "It's been so many years." His mind was jumping all around, what he'd do, what he couldn't do anymore. "Why not?"

Miguel took a snapper off the hook, passed the barb just below its dorsal fin and tossed the fish past the reef. He played his line out slowly with his left hand, the small bait fish swimming off into the tide. Then he quickly caught another and tossed that one out as well. He held a line in each hand. There were big greasy spots on the water, upswellings from below. There was a lot of bait splashing. That feeling again in his body, but stronger. It made him shiver.

Miguel leaned against the pole set in the rocks and stretched his aching legs. Even just standing these days had become painful for him. Soon he would no longer be able to climb onto these rocks, but so what? He would throw his line from the beach. Then an enormous shadow moved out from the rocks below. So big. Were his eyes playing tricks? He tried to shake his right arm back to life, but it was useless. He would need to make do without it. Something grabbed the snapper, ripping line through Miguel's left hand. A big fish was swimming offshore with the snapper in its mouth. Miguel pulled back on the line setting the hook. The fish tore off into deeper water while Miguel worked the line under the calloused heel of his foot as he'd planned, creating drag like on a fishing reel. His right hand was closed around the other handline.

The big fish ran offshore for about fifteen minutes, slowed a little by Miguel's foot. Finally, the fish stopped, hanging in the current. It was hard to pull a heavy fish in with one hand. He grabbed a few inches of line while holding hard with his foot, then grabbing the line again and pulled in a little more, then did it again, letting the line coil at his feet. Each pull bringing the fish a foot or two closer. In all the years casting from these rocks he'd never fought anything so powerful.

Then the other handline went shooting out of his right hand, the line slicing his palm like a blade. With his right hand cut and burning he couldn't hold the line. Miguel needed to take a chance. He took the handline in his left hand and cinched it around the old wooden pole stuck in the rock. If the fish sprinted away the line would break. But there was nothing else to do.

The old man switched the second fish to his left hand and began to slowly pull it back toward the rocks. The fight of this one was heavy but not so fierce. It was like doing curls, bringing the fish back a foot or two each pull. The right hand was useless now, bleeding badly with no strength at all. He pulled the fish with the left hand, inching it ahead. When his good hand would no longer grip the line, he pulled with his left elbow sometimes catching a breath by mashing the line down on the rocks with the heel of his foot. It took him almost an hour to inch the big black grouper to the rocks below. It must have weighed a hundred pounds. It was laying on the surface below him on its side, slowly moving its gills. Miguel fancied it was making eye contact. He had killed a lot of groupers in his time but always felt badly about it. They seemed friendly to him, almost human. Miguel took his knife in hand, got onto his belly and reached down to the water as close to the grouper as he could manage and cut the line. The big fish slowly swam away.

The other fish was still swimming somewhere in the darkness. Miguel went back to his line tied to the pole and began retrieving the second big fish, inch by inch while imagining what it might be. Every part of his body hurt. His good hand was cramping like a claw and the line sliced deeper into cuts on each pull. When he could no longer feel the hand, he crimped the line between his toes, tried to slow the big fish this way while massaging his hands and taking breaths. He would need his left hand to land it. He tried to shake his left hand back to life while holding on with his toes until he was afraid the taut line would cut one off.

After a half hour more there was a monster cubera snapper just below him lying on the surface. In his life on the water he'd never seen a snapper close to this size, nor had any other fisherman in Fragata. He guessed it weighed more than eighty pounds.

Miguel took the gaff in his bloody hands and laying on his belly carefully reached down six feet. He'd only have one chance. If he grazed the snapper it would run off again and he'd never find the strength to pull it back. He reached down as far as he could manage and placed the gaff through the gill behind the snapper's head.

The snapper was very heavy and Miguel was weak and exhausted. When he had it up three feet the fish thrashed with its tail, nearly pulled him off the rocks but somehow his right hand grabbed at a crevice in the rocks behind him and he saved himself. Lifting the fish onto the rocks was a huge effort. It felt like his left arm would rip out of its socket. But he got it up there.

Miguel lay exhausted for some time before hauling the cubera across the rocks and back to his house.

When Miguel finished telling his story to Rachel and the

other fishermen, he got up slowly from the beach chair. He turned to me with a tired smile and said, "*Seguro, hombre.*"

~

Late night in the lounge: "But the truth is, my sister loved him," Rachel recalled. "She couldn't get enough of Silvano and felt terrible regret about the lost years. Lavished him with kisses and stories of faraway places. She took him with her for groceries and walked with him back and forth from school. She slept with him in the same bed. They were always together. My sister was a changed woman. She wasn't interested in dancing and young lovers. He was her lover. And though it pains me, he adored her, nuzzled into her breasts, kissed her and called her 'Mommy.' Sondra was his mommy. He had his mommy. He discovered in my sister a depth of caring and love that I didn't know was there. Everyone saw it. It was beautiful and devastating for me to watch. My mother followed them around the village like a *cachorro*. He was the jewel of the family. Every soul in Fragata loved Silvano.

"My sister took him to play soccer each Saturday. Silvano was a fast runner. My sister cheered for him from the stands as if he were Pelé. Then one day he was breaking for the goal when he suddenly collapsed onto the ground. Everyone watched in alarm as he began to have a seizure. My sister ran onto the field and held him in her arms. Someone grabbed his

tongue. But after ten minutes he was okay. We drove him to the hospital in Nicoya and the doctors gave him an exam. The doctors said Silvano was okay."

~

Before bed in my little room: Rachel never wanted others to observe our affection. At night she made me leave the lounge ahead of her so late-owl neighbors wouldn't gossip she was coming back with me to my room. Was it because of our age difference or some image of independence she was fostering in the village or some other relationship she hadn't told me about? I didn't know why but it was okay. Our kissing and caresses had been ardent and satisfying to me. If our relationship was partly my illusion, I didn't want to know. Although as days passed and her story became more painful, Rachel's affection became more intermittent. I recalled the same thing happening to me long ago, when I was a writer. I'd just put everything into my work.

Sometimes Rachel revised her story, and even our story, like an author searching for the best way to steer the narrative. As her role in the family history became more tortured, she revisited her own relationship with sex. "I would like to do everything for you," she said to me one night after we'd been kissing. "But I can't. When I was giving birth to Angelo the doctor needed to cut my vagina. Then the nurse put her fingers inside me to pull Angelo out." Rachel demonstrated stretching and ripping with her hands. "She did so much damage to me. I couldn't be sexual with anyone after this. I was too wide. I was ruined."

Sad, very sad but in an odd way this news was appealing. In my little room I thought of Jake Barnes who had been ruined in the war and unable to consummate his love with Lady Brett Ashley. Jake's misfortune heightened their love and that wrenching impossibility made Hemingway's *The Sun Also Rises* larger than life.

~

A lot of the guys who worked for Extermination Power were transients looking to make a buck until they could find cleaner or easier work or until school started or until the dream job came along. Some were doing extermination briefly for drug money; there were teachers who had been laid off, failed actors, a couple of struggling painters, and now one ex-novelist, all of us waiting for the next good thing to pull us out of basements and crawl spaces. And there was Robert Stassi, a Methodist minister with two master's degrees and a PhD. I surely wouldn't have remained with Extermination Power for so many years if I hadn't met Robert Stassi, who joined our company with the handle, The Most Dangerous Man.

"I was made for this work," he said to me on one of my

first days with the company. "I arrived at this business swimming in shit. I was prepared providentially to do this work and then to wake up Sunday mornings and offer my sermon in church."

Robert's petite Asian wife had struggled with depression from the day he met her. For seven years he deeply loved her and offered the power of his faith. He took her to counselors and spiritual healers. Many times she tried to take her life and Robert managed to save her, until the day he came back from church he found her in their bathroom hanging from the shower head. For the next three years Robert wandered the city lost and suicidal himself. Much of the time he was homeless, eating out of garbage cans, until Andy offered him a job as an exterminator.

"Why did they call you the most dangerous man?" I asked.

"In any situation who is the most dangerous man?" he answered. "In a hostage situation. In any crime scene, the cops will always tell you, it's the guy who has nothing to lose. That was me the first year or two in the business. I'd fought to save my wife but I couldn't do it. I was living way below despair. I was already living with rats. Get out of my way. Killing vermin was a blast for me. I had this enormous appetite for it. And I felt invincible like John Travolta in *Saturday Night Fever*.

Robert showed me the ropes. He taught me how to survive in the business. But more than that, he understood the hilarity, the tragedy, the absurdity, and even the "art of the career" as he called it. "No one goes to high school dreaming of a career as an exterminator," he said to me one night over beers. "It chooses you." In the evenings after work we exchanged stories of the day.

My first week on the job I went to an apartment in the East Village and the problem was easy to spot even for a rank beginner. Everywhere I looked there were mouse droppings. They were all over this man's kitchen counter and on his bed, on his pillows and sheets, all over the floor, on his shoes. He was living in mice. There were beakers of chemicals all around and the guy spoke in a Russian accent. For sure he was operating a drug factory. But it was the mouse turds that got me. As if he had been breeding mice. I started throwing things around, pulling furniture off the walls, boxes filled with chemicals. All the while this guy looked uneasy. At first I thought he was nervous about the chemicals, that I was going to turn him in. I was looking for "entry points." Robert had taught me that I needed to find the little crevices and holes in the floor or walls where the mice came into the apartment. Sure enough I found several behind the furniture, and I stuffed in poison the way I'd been taught. I filled the holes with steel wool so the mice would need to eat the poison and die trapped inside the walls. But while I did this work the guy looked positively stricken. The mice were a big part of his life. I had the feeling that soon as I left, he was going to pull the steel wool out of the walls and let the mice run free.

"That's how I feel," Robert said to me over his beer. "I see them as God's creatures that have so much more in common with us than we can bear to admit. They're just trying to do what we're trying to do. Mice and rats are trying to get by. They're trying to get by in New York City. Unless you're Donald Trump, it's hard to survive here." At first, when Robert talked this way I thought he was crazy or putting me on. "You gotta eat! They want their meatball parmesan. They're trying to find companionship. The rats do that, and we do the same."

"It's so hard to catch a rat," Robert reflected. "You gotta turn a place upside down, throw furniture all over. Before I catch a loose rat, I'm sweating through my clothes and I can't catch my breath. It's a war. I'm exhausted and then I still have to kill the thing. Many times I've taken rats outside and turned them loose in the street or brought them into the subway and lowered them onto the tracks. But usually there's no time for this because of my schedule. I've killed rats in so many different ways. I'll put them in a garbage bag and whip them onto the floor. It's a very mob way of doing it. I drown them. Sometimes I strangle them. Then you realize how strong they are and how they're struggling to live. And you become an animal yourself. Things just come out of you when you're strangling a rat. Like you're finding a primitive violence in yourself you didn't know was there. Like you see a character on TV in the *Sopranos*. . . . He's not a killer but now he is a killer. He unleashes a primal savagery that's inside. You're strangling the thing and find yourself yelling and cursing. You don't even know why you're doing it until the rat stops breathing and then there's a brief calm. . . . And then the chef from the fancy restaurant rushes over to slap me on the back because I'm his hero, I've kept his place open. And I guess I'm smiling, but it's a sick smile. Because the guilt comes later and I know I'll have to deal with that.

"Look, I'll show you." Robert flipped open his cell phone and showed me pictures. He had hundreds of pictures of dead birds, roaches, and rodents. "I've had to kill a lot of things . . . I keep pictures of many of the pests I needed to kill . . . I guess as a memorial."

~

In a few more weeks the onshore winds will come with the rainy season but today the ocean is still calm. Rachel arrives with an armful of dripping wash. She looks pissed and walks by without a word. She hangs their poor wrinkled things on the picket fence without turning my way. Maybe she's growing tired of our love affair . . . but perhaps not. She comes over, gives me an absent hug as though we'd been married twenty years, and then settles on her chair. "I was Silvano's mother for nearly four years and now my sister acted like his illness, whatever it was or wasn't, was her private war." Rachel's face was pained.

I often forget she is Rachel, makes her own rules, makes fast judgments, and I have to cut her slack. When she withdraws from me for two hours or two days, I can't pull her back until she's ready, but it's hard for me to always dance to her rhythm. I once said to her, "Rachel, I always say yes to you and you almost always say no." She smiled at me, softening but not amending what we both knew was true.

"My sister's fears and regrets were bigger than life. Bigger than Silvano, whatever was wrong with him. I couldn't match it. Her needs and passions were always larger. My sister crowded out the fears we all felt. Her audacity crowded my brain. Made me angry. If I said a word or made a suggestion, she snapped at me. I hid in the lounge arguing with the pizza guy who wanted more money each week. He was making great pizza, but his salary was eating up profits.

"Silvano had another seizure walking in the village, but not so severe, only lasted a few minutes. 'It's not so bad,' I told my sister who could not stop crying. We took him back to the hospital for magnetic imaging. 'Something is crowding his brain,' said the doctor. 'But we don't know what it is. We can find nothing.'

"We hung on those words. There's nothing. But what does it mean, crowding his brain? How can nothing there be crowding the brain? . . . But let's forget about it. There's nothing there. We took Silvano to the beach. He played in the waves. He loved it right out front here," she said pointing at the small surf nearly reaching our feet.

"Then one morning Silvano met me in the lounge for breakfast and I saw that he was eating with his left hand. 'Why don't you eat with your right hand, Silvano?'

"'*No funciona*, Rachel.' He showed me the right hand would no longer open or close. He was such a calm delicate child. He gave me a hug to say his little hand was not such a big problem. '*No te preocupes*, Rachel.' He'd said this to me before when he was five when I was his mommy. It always broke my heart when he said this.

"Look at how peaceful the ocean is today," she said pointing in front of us. "The movement from perfect to catastrophe can be super fast. Like flipping the channel on the TV. Getting back to where we were seemed possible and we all tried to do that trick, Mom and me and even Sondra, who'd quieted down

for some reason. Life would just go on. It's so beautiful in this place," she said pointing out to the pristine beach and the ocean past the reef. "We tried to play it that way. I did, for sure.

"We decided to send him to the private hospital in San José, which is the best in Costa Rica, find the problem once and for all and fix it. I said to Mom and Sondra, okay, I'm going to keep working here and you guys will go to San José and take care of Silvano. Don't worry. I'll pay all the bills. Would cost a lot of money but the lounge was doing great. Tourists were coming for seafood and we had a big takeout business for pizza from the surrounding villages. I'd pay the bills and send them money for an apartment in San José while the doctors found the answer. . . . I felt bad staying here but this was my job. I wouldn't be able hold Silvano and kiss him. That wasn't my part of it.

"The doctors in San José sent the biopsy off to a hospital in Spain for analysis and it was two weeks before we learned that Silvano had a very unusual cancer, deep in his brain. It was inoperable. But the doctors assured us the cancer was very slow growing. Silvano would live a good life for four or five years, maybe longer. We'd have five years to love our wonderful boy. We'd make the years a celebration, wonderful meals in the lounge, beach parties. We'd take him to rodeos. We could slow time with our love. And they said, maybe we'd have him longer. Maybe there would be a new drug—there were always new cures on the horizon. We'd been so alarmed for Silvano that now a slow growing cancer seemed like a holiday."

~

As Rachel's story grew more intense, I remembered the feeling from decades earlier when I'd first glimpsed the ending of a story I'd been struggling to get right. I was so excited and grateful that the foreground of my own life all but disappeared. I recalled the increasing frustration of my poor wife who couldn't reach me though she tried, and how little that mattered to me. And now I was starting to feel that Rachel's story was crowding me out. Her tragedy was initiating my own. Some mornings I would ask her to tell me about a sequence of events we'd already discussed. I needed more details, more color. Actually, I was stalling for time before the end, more mornings to sit on the beach holding her hand, more late nights in the lounge.

Where would the end of her story leave me? For Rachel, I was a novelist and it would soon be my job to go off and write the thing. I couldn't just stick around here fishing with Miguel from the rocks. I'd be a sixty-five-year-old man hanging around the lounge in the evening hoping for a smile. I'd be less valuable than the old man who came by in the mornings to put out the beach umbrellas.

Impulsively I told Rachel that I needed to go back to New

York for business. The idea had just hit me that I needed to get away from her. Remaining here was like rushing to the edge of a cliff. A separation might work to my advantage. Maybe she would realize that I'd brought something into her life that she didn't want to give up.

Rachel wasn't at all surprised. I was afraid she would ask me, what was my pressing business in New York but she filled in this information herself. "Will you have a meeting with your publisher?" I nodded yes and hoped she wouldn't ask if I would mention her story. This lie was swallowing me alive. But there were no more questions.

"You'll miss me," she said leaving her beach chair to prepare the fish and shrimps for lunch.

"You'll miss me." I thought about that on the plane back to the New York. It made me smile. That was the closest that Rachel could come to saying, "I'll miss you."

~

Monday morning, I called Andy in the office, told him I was back in the city and asked if he could use an extra man for the next three or four weeks. I knew he'd say yes. Andy and I got along. During the football season we frequently exchanged remarks about the absurdity of being New York Jets fans. Andy didn't quite appreciate the grandeur of losing like Robert and me and he frequently gave us his two season tickets to watch the game in Jersey. Andy was the boss but he seemed to appreciate Robert's other worldly vision of their work. He knew Robert was one of a kind.

My first morning back on the job I visited a couple of monthly clients, setting out mouse traps and poison for roaches. I was surprised by how pleasant it felt doing the work. The feel of my gear in the bag was so familiar, I could pull out different traps and poisons or my rubber hammer or gloves without looking. From the basements and crawl spaces where I worked Fragata seemed so far away, as if I'd concocted the whole fantasy.

In the afternoon I got a call from the office and was sent to a woman in Queens who had rats in her basement. I went down there and threw around boxes and assorted knickknacks for half an hour until I found a rat hiding in a corner. When it turned my way, the sight of it made me jump. The rat only had half a face. It had lost one eye and I could see into its mandible and brain. Surely it had tried to eat cheese from a snap trap and half its face had been sheared off, but it hadn't killed him. I would have set out some poison, and left for home but I thought of Robert, the way he'd feel about this rat who'd taken the kind of a hit that would make most of us go down for the count. I left him alone, went back upstairs and told the woman I couldn't find any rats.

I couldn't wait to tell Robert about the one with half a face. We met at our favorite Italian restaurant on Bleecker Street that features excellent pasta and cheap carafes of red wine to keep stories flowing. Robert was wearing a cast on his wrist.

"I almost got whacked couple weeks ago," he said in the flat it-don't-really-matter-man style of narration perfectly suited to his sensibility. My friend has learned to survive and even prosper in a region between the living and the dead. The voices of his dead wife along with creatures he's killed have become his conscience as well as his muses in the music he composes and plays on his guitar.

"I was called to a restaurant in the West Village," continued Robert. "An A-list actress was eating dinner and she saw a water bug walking across the table. She ran out of the place and the following morning the story was in the *Post* and the *Daily News*. The owner was in a panic about his business and I was called in. I spent two hours crawling under booths and tables and couldn't find a single bug. I would have left but the owner pleaded with me to keep looking. I located a crawl space above the ceiling with access from the kitchen and I decided to take a look. I went up there with my flashlight and started edging ahead. There was absolutely no headroom. I'm pulling my bag along with my left hand, my mouth practically on the floor. I was moving ahead which was wrenching my neck and then I spot a bug crawling ahead of me. I followed it with the flashlight hoping to find its nest. I inched ahead dropping the bag but grabbing my rubber hammer with my left hand . . . and I'm considering the absurdity of my situation . . .

I'm a Methodist minister with three graduate degrees and I'm sweating and getting tangled in electrical wires for this bug. Then just when I'm getting close enough to smash it, I crawl over a trap door which gives way and I fall headfirst eight feet down into the kitchen sink filled with pots and pans in soapy water. I got lucky fending off with my arm. It could have been my head. I could have died for a water bug."

Back in the city, there were wonderful Robert evenings of music and wine with inspiring tales of hunting in elevator shafts and basements and hilarity about the coming NFL season. We both lived and died for the Jets on Sundays, and over the years mostly we died and headed into work on Mondays hungover with defeat.

Robert is no Segovia but his guitar playing is a strong rocking dirge sound infused with passages of tenderness. The feeling it evokes is wrenching and it stays with you. He told me "the very instant I was cutting my wife down from the shower I was making wailing sounds, a kind of strange suffering music, and I knew I needed to buy a guitar and learn to play."

Two or three evenings a week, after the rest of the guys have left the office, he brings his guitar into the tiny, two-stall bathroom down the hall from Andy's office. Robert likes to wear his exterminator uniform when he plays including knee pads and mask, so I wear mine as well. We settle on the toilets, and I accompany him laying down rhythms on the bongos. My favorites are "Captain Cockroach" and "Rodenti-cide," and though his lyrics are often about rats and bugs, the feelings evoked tug at the heart, I guess because Robert cares so much about these creatures. My artist mother would have called Robert's music legitimate. We usually play his songs for a half hour or so in the bathroom stalls before heading home. Once or twice a month Robert plays in a bar solo on Friday or Saturday night, always with a rat trap attached to the head of his guitar and sometimes he wears his mask. But I only play with him in the bathroom.

~

I enjoyed my weeks in New York working at the job and spending many evenings hanging out with Robert. I had lived this way for years, and there was no stretch or pretending. In three more weeks the NFL season would begin and I found myself looking forward to it. But still I missed Rachel and wanted to go back.

Each night before bed I sent her a text message describing something about the city or about playing music with Robert, but without ever mentioning the kind of work we do. Mostly she didn't answer but two or three times she responded, "good" or "goodnight." A few of my texts were ardent love notes. I asked her to send me a photograph of herself and she didn't answer. I asked many questions about her state of mind and the news in Fragata, and she never answered one of these. I tried to imagine what she was doing.

This lady who is such a storyteller, so verbal and nuanced on the beach, had gone silent, which made me think the whole love affair, the entire whacky scene in Costa Rica with Sylvia's magic and Sondra watching Rachel and me from the shadows, was in my head, like Robert having regular conversations with his dead wife. But I kept writing her the notes and dreamed of holding her in my arms.

One night in the john we played a new composition, "Maggot's Plight." There was a lot of Dylan in this one. Robert loved Dylan. His strumming kept building and by the end it sounded like a rocking dirge. I think it was the best we ever played together, and we were both feeling a little thrilled. When we headed back to Andy's office with the instruments, Robert asked if I wanted to see his blog. He'd never offered to show it to me before. Maybe now because I'd told Robert some things about Rachel, how I was crazy about her but she was walled off, and I didn't know if I could ever get inside. . . . Of course, I wanted to see it.

Robert's blog was mostly jarring and unusually posed photographs of a mummified cat having a series of difficult conversations with a mummified rat.

"I don't want to be prevented by you. I need to die. I want to die." said Rose, his dead wife who is embodied in a rat floating upside down in a toilet. "It's supposed to happen. By you keeping me here you are prolonging my pain. You're preventing my loved ones from finding relief in a new life where they are no longer burdened by my depression and suicide attempts. Taking it upon yourself to stop everyone from committing suicide is incredibly myopic and presumptuous."

"When I come home from work, before I even put my bag down or take my coat off, I walk over to the bedroom and check to see if you're there," answers the mummified cat, Robert, who is smoking a cigarette. "I'm still grieving that you're not there . . . And I'm so relieved that you're not there. . . ."

"Nobody ever plans to write a blog about a dead cat and a dead rat and make them talk about the rat's suicide," Robert remarked, while I scrolled through the portraits and conversations. "It just came out of me like the music does. My wife was in such a dark place for most of our time together. She couldn't really ask how I was doing when she was alive because she was so depressed. But I'm sure she would have liked to know, if she could have asked.

"Rose was making attempts on her life, one after another, but she was still my best friend. And all of a sudden, she's gone and I have no one to talk to. No real friends. These characters became my friends and became a way to have conversations with her. She was the rat and I was the cat. The cat feels responsible for the rat's death. But the cat is also dead. Because I was dead. A dead man talking to his dead wife."

For years the blog meant everything to Robert and he lived in fear that it would somehow become lost on the internet and he would lose this connection with her, and then he'd be lost. The actors themselves, the mummified cat and rat were found in an abandoned synagogue in the Bronx, which was then renovated and became the church that Robert presently pastors.

"I recognized the total absurdity of these dialogues," Robert admitted, "even when I was composing them, but they helped me get on my feet. One time I was in the apartment of a woman on the Upper West Side making a service call and we got to talking. We just clicked, or that's how it felt to me, you know, like strangers on a train. And I really opened up to her, told her that I used to be a pastor of a church before my wife committed suicide and mentioned these conversations that I still have with Rose. The lady took this in. After a moment, she answered. 'Well, you're a really good exterminator.'"

Here is the entry in Robert's blog that stays with me to this day: "You will mourn me forever." Rose, the dead rat, says to Robert, "and you will wish you could have killed me before we ever met."

I don't think Robert's blog would have registered so high on my sanity scale before my time with Rachel. Almost certainly that's why Robert waited so long to show it to me. Before falling asleep that night I wrote her a text.

"You know I've opened my heart to u Rachel. I greatly look forward to coming back to see u. I dream about it. If you decide you don't care for me anymore than u need to tell me. It's not fair not to tell me."

Rachel didn't answer. I might have guessed. I'd already paid for my ticket to Costa Rica. I debated for two days whether I should just forget the ticket and stay in New York.

But it wasn't a real debate. She had this irresistible pull, even in her silence, like Rose the rat. On Monday morning I would fly back to Costa Rica.

Friday was my last day on the job. I was on my way to one of my regular customers when I got a text from Andy there was a rodent issue in a high-end Upper East Side restaurant. I went into the swanky place wearing leather gloves while lunch customers were beginning to arrive. Two waitresses whispered to me that the rat was on the other side of the restaurant and they led me to an elegant corner banquet set up. I got on the floor and fished out the rat with a coat hanger. When it came out the waitresses screamed and ran which caused eight or ten customers to stand up and point at the rat, which just sat out in the open staring at me, considering its fate. I slugged it with

my rubber mallet, stunning it. I realized then that I'd forgotten to bring my canvas bag. All eyes were on me while I looked for someplace to put the rat. I heard a murmur when I picked it up with my gloved hand.

I was stuck in place for a moment or two considering what to do with it. I could feel so much aversion coming my way. Most exterminators prefer to poison rats, myself included, but this was not one of those situations. I thought of Robert who always tried to avoid using poison. He said that feeding rats poisoned baits is an act of deception. Poisons used today are anti-coagulants making the rats bloat up and bleed out from their orifices, a horrible slow death.

While I considered my next move, the rat began to squirm in my hand and I could hear the building murmur of unease all around. I couldn't think of any other solution, so I walked through the restaurant holding it in my hand. On the sidewalk I turned toward the entryway of a building and strangled the creature while it fought to stay alive. I knew it was the right thing to do, but still, strangling a rat messes you up.

~

On Sunday morning I realized I'd forgotten to buy Rachel a present. What an idiot! Before leaving for New York I'd spent hours trying to decide what would surprise and delight her. It was my plan to shop in the best boutiques and perfume shops in Manhattan. I knew that she liked hand cream. Maybe I'd buy her the best hand cream in the world, something that Ivanka Trump would use. Luckily, Macy's is open on Sundays.

I arrived at Macy's around 9 a.m. and discovered the place was locked up, didn't open until ten. I sat on a fire hydrant beside a couple of homeless guys sleeping on cardboard. For the next hour I thought about the futility of flying back to Costa Rica and about hand creams, which I know nothing about, and then actually imagining that the right choice of hand cream would tip the balance in my favor. You can fall into a certain way of thinking, like Robert conferring with a rat who is his dead wife, and no one is going to convince you that you're wrong. On the fire hydrant in front of Macy's, love itself seemed to hang on my choice of hand creams.

Finally, I was inside the department store charging from counter to counter asking each sales lady which of the creams was the best in the world. Each had a different suggestion. Each of the creams felt terrific on my hands. I went back and forth, an impossible choice really. I decided by price and bought three of them, La Mer, RestorSea, and CrabTree & Evelyn, each of the tubes cost nearly a hundred dollars. No girl in Costa Rica had ever had such hand creams. I bought her a big box of Godiva chocolates on the way out.

In spite of evenings with Robert and relishing my favorite New York restaurants and museums, and nearly a month without Rachel answering my texts, I was desperate to get back to her, hold her hand on the beach, kiss her, listen to her story, start up the machine of our romance, see where it would lead.

~

My first morning back at the lounge was overcast with storm clouds gathering over the mountains. It was windy and spitting rain. I arrived at our beach chairs, positioned myself on the ruined cushions, and took the brown plastic bag with the hand creams and set it on the sand beside me. So stupid. I'd left Macy's without having her presents beautifully gift wrapped. After a half hour I was wondering if Rachel would show up. She had often made me wait, but never this long. When she arrived finally, she wore a bitter expression that matched the stormy weather.

"I'm so sick of this place," she said before sitting. "I don't want to worry about it anymore . . . I need to get out of here."

I was completely thrown by this. Was Rachel offering some oblique invitation that I should save her from stormy nights sleeping on top of the bar?

But how could I bring her to New York for Robert's bathroom concerts and our shoptalk of roaches and rats? What would she make of it?

Craziness was coursing through my brain and without thinking I felt for the plastic bag and handed it to her without explanation.

"What is this?" she said looking inside. "What are they?"

"Hand creams. They're the best in the world," I said idiotically.

She held the tubes in her hand, considering each of them. I'd left the price tag on the tubes so she would see they were the best in the world. But it wasn't the smoothest idea.

"You spent three hundred dollars on hand creams?" She shook her head incredulously. "Three hundred dollars? Do you realize I haven't served one lunch in the last four days? We haven't made three hundred dollars this month! Hand creams?"

Rachel gestured at the emptiness of the Fragata Lounge. With a blackening sky and rain clouds approaching quickly from the mountains, the place looked more forlorn than I'd remembered. It was the beginning of the rainy season.

"I want someone else to take responsibility for this place," she said bitterly while stuffing the hand creams back in the plastic bag and dropping it onto the wet sand. "When I took over the lounge from Mom everything was going great. I had time for myself. I was surfing, relaxing. After lunch I would take a run on the beach. I was making so much I closed the place on Mondays and took my motorcycle to Marbella or one of the other beaches. . . . Today my mom and sister never ask, how are you Rachel? Why do you look sad? Whenever they come, they ask for money. Whatever I have for them is never enough. They act like I'm stealing and living rich."

"But you keep the family going."

"I just don't care anymore," she went on. "For years I worried, what will I do if the fisherman doesn't bring the shrimps? What a laugh! What good did the shrimps do me? If we don't have avocados for guacamole, so what, fuck 'em."

By now it was raining hard and there was lightning all around. Rachel's hair was drenched and she looked haggard and years older. "Please, let this place blow out to sea in the next storm . . . I gotta get outta here before I'm old and dead."

But where could I take her? She'd be expecting book parties and glamour.

It was beginning to pour.

The plastic bag was laying on the wet sand like beach trash. I wondered if she'd remember to pick it up or leave it to wash away with the high tide.

"Could you really leave this place? It's part of who you are?"

"Sí"

Time to race for cover. Rachel grabbed the plastic bag and we ran inside the lounge.

Sondra was already in the kitchen furiously cleaning fish. After a quick word with her sister, Rachel turned back to me. "There are two couples driving up for lunch from Nicoya," she told me with a bounce of optimism. "Thanks," she said lifting the plastic bag.

That saved the day for me. Maybe I could bring her back to New York. Rachel spun me like a top.

~

Mornings on the beach were now windy and rain was always hanging over the mountains. I liked Fragata better without the relentless sun. It was cool and felt like there were chances that hadn't been considered.

"Where were we?" Rachel asked after settling into her beach chair.

"You last told me that you believed you could slow time if you loved Silvano enough. That you were making a beautiful life for him."

She nodded.

"*Es verdad*. It was a beautiful life. We came to the beach every morning. All the kids came to see our boy. Sondra and I made big picnic lunches, all the treats he enjoyed. Each day was a celebration. My mom was happy. It's the only time I can remember Mommy being happy. She's always wanted more, better. *Una vida major*. She resented when he came into the world because he almost killed her daughter, but now he was her precious grandson. We knew we had him for five more years.

"Silvano was an early riser and often he met me in the morning for breakfast while his mom slept in. About two weeks after returning from the hospital in San José, Silvano came by the lounge when I was just waking up. He put his face next to mine and tried to say good morning, but the words 'planes' and 'horses' came out of his mouth. I'll never forget planes and horses. He couldn't understand why he was saying these words and he cried a little. So did I. I tried to tell him not to worry, but no words came out of my mouth.

"The treatments would cost a lot. They'd need to rent a house in San José near the hospital. Again I told them I'd take care of the bills but even with our pizza business I worried it wouldn't be enough. Silvano could still walk a little by holding the walls but any effort at all made him tired.

"We threw a party for him on the soccer field hoping to raise money for his treatments. But maybe the fresh green grass of the field wasn't the best setting for our tragedy. Also, that afternoon Silvano looked happy and full of energy around his friends like he could still break free and score the winning goal. Our neighbors began talking shit. 'He's not that bad.' 'Look at him.' 'Nothing's wrong.' They thought we were rich people because we owned the lounge and we just wanted to take their money. Silvano walked through their gossip like a saint. I swear he glowed. 'You guys are making all that stuff up,' some asshole said to me. I wanted to kick him in the balls.

"A couple of mornings Silvano was able to say the right words and then our hearts soared. We could take a breath and grasped at what the doctors promised just two weeks earlier— we had him five more years.

"'Mama, I love you more than I'm afraid of death. I'm always gonna be with you.'

"'Stop this talk, Silvano. *Tu no vas a morir.*' We said this like a chorus and Silvano answered with his beautiful sad smile.

"They promised us five more years. We repeated that like a prayer."

~

A chilly overcast morning in front of the lounge: "We all knew what was coming," Rachel recalled. "Two days before leaving for the hospital in San José, Sondra, Mom, and I decided to cut off our hair to be with him—so we'd all look the same. I drove my motorcycle to a woman who had a shop in another village and told her, 'Cut it off, all of it.' She looked at me like I was a crazy woman. My hair then was below my ass. I hadn't cut it in ten years. It was my most beautiful part. But this lady who knew me a little thought I was just tired of having long hair and started to cut it to my shoulder. 'You'll look great this way,' she told me. I got so pissed. 'All of it off. Didn't you hear me! Nothing! No hair!' She shook her head; no. Decided I must be a crazy lady. So I took the scissors from her and started chopping. When I looked like a scarecrow, she said, okay, okay, and finished the job. Then she shaved me bald.

"Later that night when I saw Mom and Sondra, they hadn't

cut their hair. They said they hadn't had time and would do it in San José. I knew they wouldn't. But I felt happy that he and I would be together in this way.

"So the three of them left on the bus for San José. I was here working. That was my job. Pay the bills. Send money. I didn't have the time to go to him, hold him in my arms while he was getting treatments. My sister called me six, eight times each day. 'He vomited all the way in the bus.' 'Silvano don't breathe right.' Then she hung up and I'd try to call her back, four, five times. Nothing. Nothing. No answer.

"She would call while I was serving customers, screaming at me. Then she'd hang up. Call back ten minutes later and couldn't stop crying.

"'What's wrong Sondra? Speak to me.' She'd hang up the phone.

"I was trying to run the restaurant. 'Rachel, most of his brain has the cancer. He's talking nonsense.' I'm trying to smile for my customers. For the first time in a month twenty people came for lunch from one of the hotels. People drove all this way to eat and be happy. They don't want to see a crying woman. '*Smile, Rachel.*' I tried to smile.

"She said such things to me. 'You never cared about Silvano. You don't know what he's going through.'

"I couldn't catch my breath. '*Breathe Rachel.*'

"It's true, I wasn't there. They needed more money for chemo, for radiation. My pizza guy demanded I triple his salary. I couldn't pay it so I let him go. A mistake, a terrible, terrible mistake. 'Leave, just leave, I told him. I can't afford to pay you.' Now he was gone.

"Customers were coming from other villages for pizza. 'Oh my god, you don't have pizza?' 'What happened to the pizza?' So they walked out. 'He's dying, Rachel. Silvano can't breathe.'

"'*Breathe, Rachel.*'

"Every day my sister screamed at me and then hung up the phone. 'You haven't been one night in the hospital with him . . . he no longer speaks. You never loved him.'

"She was crazy. I was crazy.

"'Silvano had a heart attack.' She cursed me and hung up. I tried to smile to my customers, catch my breath. She called back. 'He's gonna die, Rachel.'

"I am a person who needs to be loved. I can't be screamed at. I kept working, trying to make the money. It was never enough. No one ever asked me if I was tired. 'Why don't you send the money!! What's wrong with you?'

"There was no money.

"'He's dying, Rachel. Silvano is dying.' My sister was weeping and cursing me. I was trying to be pleasant for the lunch customers. They were all we had. No one wants to hear about a kid dying while they are eating their shrimps. There was no more money to send. I shouldn't have fired the pizza guy.

"'Where's Mom?' I asked Sondra. 'Put her on the phone!'

"'She went to Nicaragua.'

"Oh Mom."

~

On a chilly night in Fragata Lounge, I waited while Rachel cleaned up after dinner. Sondra was around more than I'd remembered from my first trip here, some nights washing dinner dishes with a seething expression that cried, I wasn't put on earth for this work. A few times she nodded hello but more often she scowled or looked right through me. One evening I was surprised to notice she was using one of the hand creams I had given to her sister. I didn't mention it to Rachel. These two were closer than I could have imagined.

"Mother brought a message back from Sylvia," Rachel pushed on as if talking to herself or to a priest. "Silvano needs to be fed poison from a scorpion and the poison from a rattlesnake. She promised it was the only way to save him."

"What? Did you try to stop this crazy talk?"

Rachel ignored this remark, looking past me.

"Sylvia said it would be very expensive to get these things but was the only way. He must have both poisons and they need to be taken together. It was the only way to save his life. My sister believed her."

"But you didn't believe this."

"Look," Rachel said staring straight at me, "His body was

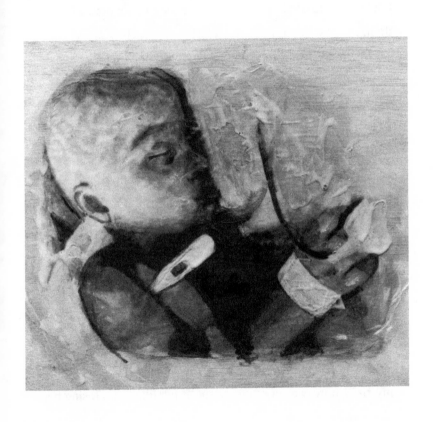

shutting down. He couldn't eat or talk. It was a chance. Hope is the last thing you lose in a hospital.

"I said to Sondra, 'The poisons might interfere with the drugs he's taking, a lot of drugs. You need to ask his doctors,' but Sondra insisted, 'No, no, because they're not gonna let me do it. . . . Just get it, Rachel. Get it!'"

My mind went to poisoning rats. It had been such a big part of my own life for so long, balancing the neatness of poisoning the creatures and letting them rot behind the walls with Robert's aversion and his argument for killing them quickly with his hands. There is no neat analogy here but it's where I went after many years using poisons and feeling repulsed by it. Rachel's response to her sister's urgings surprised the hell out of me. I expected she would have felt disgust and horror for her mom's sorcery and her sister going along, but no. She just rode with it.

"Sondra had a lot of hope and faith and I didn't want to crush it, because it was the only thing keeping her alive.

"It was my job to find these things and I tried not to think too much. It was my chance to help him. Or maybe helping my sister now was more important. It felt like I was losing her along with Silvano.

"'Okay,' I told my sister, 'We gonna try it.'

"I asked people in every village around here where to get the stuff. Some thought I was nuts. But others heard I was looking and sought me out. When you are in this kind of situation people just appear at your door, trying to take advantage of your pain. 'Look, I have this. It will save him.'

"I visited an old woman who lived on a remote farm. She had poison from another kind of snake. She promised it would work, but I didn't believe her. We were running out of time. I heard about an old man high in the mountains forty miles from here. I rode to him on a friend's motorcycle. He had many things in vials and bottles including both poisons. He told me, exactly what to do. Silvano needed to have eight drops of each, two times a day. I bought two little vials for five hundred dollars each. It was all the money I could get begging from everyone I knew."

Maybe it was crazy love, but I admired her for it. They had tried everything else and he was dying and just maybe Sylvia knew something the doctors didn't know. What did they have to lose? Rachel's world did not operate within the mores and science of Sloan Kettering. Sylvia had said that this cure was used all over Central America. She said it was the only chance. How could someone from the outside judge their magic and morality? It was a chance.

They gave it a shot. Sondra fed Silvano the poison twice a day for a week and they never mentioned it to the doctors. Why not, rats and children. Like Robert says, we're all God's creatures.

It didn't work.

"Something killed him," she said. "I don't know if it

was the cancer or the poison we fed him. It doesn't matter, does it?"

I shook my head no, it doesn't matter.

"What did the doctors know?" she said bitterly. "They promised us five years and our boy died in less than a month."

I gave her a big hug. We were done for the night. Rachel had fallen headfirst into the tragedy of her family. It was not a time for making love, and I'd been thinking maybe we'd passed to the other side of our romance so I was surprised at the end of this saddest chapter when Rachel pulled me close and offered her beautiful kisses until it was time for lip gloss and then to my delight she used a dab of one of the best hand creams and gave me a good night hug.

～

Unless there was steady rain, I spent afternoons on the rocks with Miguel casting my line. It had been six weeks since his battles with the big grouper and the eighty-pound cubera snapper. I had the sense my mostly silent friend hadn't enjoyed his renewed celebrity in the village. Miguel hadn't been top gun here for decades, and it was uncomfortable for him to retell his life and death battle with the cubera snapper. Talking about that tremendous catch filled him with sadness—he should have let it live. The good thing is, with time fishing stories quickly become lost in a confusion of memory and fable.

People forget, and even now in the village Miguel was again just an old man passing afternoons on the rocks tossing out his handline.

I could relate to his confusion and distress. I'd lived inside my friend Robert's world for many years after I'd been a writer. We killed vermin and wore our New York Jets jackets to the games on chilly Sunday afternoons using Andy's season tickets. We talked about painting, religion, and remorse, played music together, laughed, and somehow the vermin fit into much of it. There were so many stories and habits and great laughs through the years. That was who I had become and the earlier years of hunting for glory as a writer had lost the bitterness and bite of pain.

Robert had made peace with his tragedy, had turned it into music, Sunday sermons, and the blog. Our friendship had been a steadying force in my life. But here I was back on the precipice with Rachel, always afraid I'd get found out as a liar and fraud. Even with her delicious kisses, the density of Rachel's story made me feel more like an outsider. More and more I'd been wondering, was this lounge really my Smuggler's Rest? Rachel was here, in front of me, telling her story but I couldn't quite grasp her, though I tried each night. I wanted to pull her my way and sometimes she allowed it, like a taste, because that enabled her story, which tormented and enriched her and now teased her with a golden future, to actually have her story written and appreciated by many.

I recalled what it felt like when I was researching a character for a feature piece or a novel thirty years earlier, the man or woman before me, whom I hardly knew, unburdening intimacies as though we were lifelong buddies. "I've never told anyone this before" or "You know, you're like a shrink." I'd often heard remarks like this as we took a long evening walk along the water or sat in a dim bar over drinks, with the lush painful story of his or her life pouring out, creating deep, shared emotion. We were both touched by this moment of making something together and my stories often began with a built-in pledge of future friendship and fealty to the told story.

Later, when the talking part was over and I sat and began to type, the holy story inevitably became mine, not that I planned it that way. It happened rather quickly, without malice or forethought and without a twinge of remorse. The purity of my vision, whether I'd turned my character degrees saintly or malignant or just barely tweaked him or her, was the only truth that mattered to me when I was writing and creating the story, the story beneath the story as I sometimes called it, was everything to me. And the shared soulful evening in the dimly lit bar was long forgotten. Now Rachel was playing this game with me. But she was a better player than I ever was.

One day I asked her, "Do you have secrets?"

"Of course I have secrets. Everyone has secrets," she said

flirtatiously slamming the door. Was there something of a threat to her assertion, the intimation of a life plan she would never reveal? Or was she baiting me like a rat?

I loved her, but was there room for me inside her world with Sondra and her mother and Angelo and Silvano and the lounge and this story that obsessed her? Maybe this was just a pinprick of time and I needed to accept our strange love for what it was. But I couldn't. I couldn't give her up. I kept trying to hold her, grasping for my life.

~

Our mornings on the beach were over. It was rainy and cold. Too cold for María José's beach visits and for Sondra to walk the water's edge in her bikini. Too rainy and cold to fish on the rocks. I was frittering days until evenings when I'd meet Rachel in the lounge until we reached the end of her story—it was almost to the end.

"We drove his body to the cemetery in Nicoya, crying, holding my sister," Rachel continued. "The place was packed with people we knew and many we didn't. Little children were hugging one another. After many nice words the children let their balloons fly into the air. So many hands pointed to the sky of balloons. Then everyone left for home. You just have a feeling, now what? I had a reason to work really hard, but now? Sondra was lost, muttering to herself. My mom. I don't know what she felt. I never understood her.

"I tried to be close to my sister all the time. I told friends I'm doing my best for her, but now I'm not sure this is true because I myself was lost. During the day, we went to eat something but she couldn't eat. Just looking at the food. I knew what she's thinking. 'I gonna kill myself to be with him.'

"Then one of Sondra's close friends said, okay, why don't we go to my house. So my sister left the village with her friend for Samara. She didn't say a word to me, just left. Sondra put me on the side without even goodbye. I had promised Silvano I would take care of his mom, but she was gone. Just me and Mom looking around the empty lounge."

"You must have been confused."

"Not confused. I had to be with her. No other possibility had meaning. I took a bus to Samara and moved into the house without asking anyone's permission. When I got to the house I found her sitting on the floor in a corner, crying and holding her knees. She wouldn't let me touch her and when I said something, she shook her head, no. Everyone who visited was concerned. I slept on the floor beside her bed where I could hear her breathing. I told myself I needed to take care of my sister otherwise she will hurt herself. I believed this was true, but I had nowhere else to go. I was like a little doggy, following behind.

"We tried to make sure she was never alone.

"Her new boyfriend arrived on his motor bike from Fragata. He was much younger than my sister, really just a boy. He worked as a mate on one of the fishing boats. He stayed in Samara with us for five days. They slept together on the bed, beside me, and her child lover had endless energy for my sister who cried while they fucked. The kid didn't seem to notice or care.

"When he left, I moved into the bed with her. It was so nice to be close, to hear her breathing, to smell her. One night in my sleep I could feel her holding me tight, wrapping her big legs around my body. It was so strange for Sondra to do this. But if she wanted, it was okay. I would go anywhere with her. Sondra caressed my bald head with her hand. She began to kiss my lips and then I kissed her deeply. It was the first good thing in so long. It felt nice. I felt loved.

"Then my sister opened her eyes and looked stricken. She shoved me away, went to the other side of the bed. She whispered, 'I thought you were Silvano.'"

"When we returned to the village my sister no longer brushed her hair or washed her clothes. She smelled. She sat on one of those stools for hours drinking and talking to herself," Rachel said pointing across from us to the bar. "'*Quiero morir*, I wanna die.' She was living in another world. I couldn't reach her. Mommy sat over there in the corner looking at a fashion magazine. I knew that in a few days or a week she would disappear with her seaman boyfriend. I wouldn't hear from her for weeks until she needed money.

"Sondra always wanted to live free and wild. She ran away from her little boy when he was five years old and now Silvano had left her. 'Why doesn't God take me with him?' she'd ask me. 'If I kill myself, will I see him again?'

"When I could no longer bear to listen, Sondra went into the street, '*Me voy a matar*' she told neighbors and drunks. She called girlfriends and old lovers on the phone, 'I gonna kill myself.'

"Every hour I ran from the lounge to her little room down the road to check on her.

"One night her door was locked so I broke a window. When I walked into her bedroom she was grinning at me. Sondra was too happy to see me and I knew something was wrong. 'What the hell is going on?' I pulled the sheets off her and my sister was covered in blood. She'd slit her wrists with an exacto knife.

"Sondra, you're gonna go to hell if you do that. You'll never see him," I said to her on the way to the hospital.

"But she didn't care what I said. I took every knife from her kitchen, I took her nail files, scissors, anything she could cut with.

"She had made up her mind. Another night I came to her

place and all the lights were out. I found her on the living room floor crying and cursing. She'd tried to hang herself with a sash from her bathrobe tied to a pipe in the ceiling. The sash tore from her weight and she broke her elbow.

"'Rachel, why doesn't God take me with him?' she asked the same pitiful question as if she just thought of it for the first time.

"I'd used all the arguments I had but the last one. I knew I was gonna lose her. She'd do it again and I wouldn't be on time to save her. I held her in my arms and said, 'Sondra. Let's make another baby. I'll make the next one. It'll be your baby or if you want, it'll be our baby. We'll share it. Two moms. Or it'll be all yours. You can decide. It'll be a wonderful little boy. I think it'll be a boy.' She looked at me like I'd proposed a miracle. We both cried at the idea of our new baby to save our family.

"We'd call him, Angelo."

~

Late in the Fragata Lounge: It was the first and only night I saw Rachel wearing a sleeveless summer dress. She looked beautiful, enchanting. Rachel always choreographed our moments, set the limits, knew the right timing and things to talk about. Maybe this was how she wanted me to remember her. We were nearing the end of the story.

"When will you leave for New York?" She asked me.

"I feel like I just got here."

She laughed recalling I'd answered her same question the same way soon after I'd first arrived. "Tell me about New York. Tell me about where you live and where you write. Tell me about the wonderful restaurants you go to and the smart friends you talk to. Tell me about this new book you will write. Do you know yet how it will end?"

I hated telling her lies. I could feel my face flush. What lie should I begin with?

Rachel began to kiss me right then as if possessed by some vagrant urge. It was just the start of our evening, not the usual time for kissing. But Rachel always called the shots. She was kissing me more urgently than ever before, as if she wanted this moment to have no borders. And then she pulled her dress up over her head. She was so beautiful. Firm small breasts and strong arms, her stomach almost gone from Angelo, long athletic legs with the tattoo of Silvano's baby foot almost touching her shaved pubis, her knee rubbing softly against my groin while we kissed. I was struggling to get my pants off while she laid back on the broad bench, raised her knees and opened herself. She was salty and wet and delicious and she stretched like a cat and laughed a little while I tasted her. I was happy where I was but she pulled me back to her and began urgent kissing while playing with my balls.

Then I heard something, maybe someone behind me. I twisted my head around and there was Sondra, not ten feet away, standing in the darkened companionway of the kitchen, hands on her hips, watching.

"Your sister."

"Doesn't matter," Rachel said in a husky voice. "Shhh-hhh." She put her finger to my mouth.

I was too excited to care much. She took me in her hand and pushed me inside. Rachel had a beautiful vagina, tight and slippery, not injured at all. She was wild with me, unrestrained for the first time, or perhaps released, with Sondra watching. "Don't stop," she said to me when I slowed down, so I didn't, even though I was rounding the corner. I wanted to stay inside her for the night or at least for an hour, but I started to come and she laughed and then began to kiss me and wouldn't stop until I needed to take a breath. I put my arms around her and we stayed this way on the bench for a long time feeling grateful while we listened to the surf.

But later in my little room when I couldn't sleep, I wondered had Rachel orchestrated this night to make her sister jealous or was it to excite their infinity of passions—or perhaps she had planned Sondra's visit so I'd put it in the book—it was such a preposterous and splendid touch. As I've said, she was a remarkable story maker, a natural. She understood literary conventions without ever having studied them. I could never have imagined the Sondra moment. But also it had me wincing. The attractions in this family were gnarled and uncanny. It was our most passionate night but how much of it had to do with me? How could I ever work my way into their tight webbing.

~

The last night in the Fragata Lounge: Rachel's story was almost to the end and then she wouldn't want me to see her hanging her sorrowful laundry on the fence with chickens and land crabs underfoot, cleaning a few shrimps if there happened to be a lunch customer, serving a beer at closing to the same drunk fisherman who always tried to sneak in a feel. Rachel wanted to be the woman in the story. . . . It was wrenching. I'd have to leave.

"There was a guy I would sometimes see who lived in a nearby village," she continued. "A few times we did something together, mostly out of boredom. We fought a lot over money but sometimes he was sweet to me. I moved into his apartment for a while but there was no need to because I realized I was pregnant after the first week trying with him."

"My sister was a changed woman. There was no more talk of suicide. She was back walking the beach spilling out of her tiny bikini, going to parties at night. I'd found the right medicine this time.

"She was Sondra again, like a light switched back on. She started seeing a guy who owned the biggest club in Nicoya, who came for her a few nights a week in a fancy car. 'I'm your fun number one,' she said to him just like when she was sixteen years old. She laughed when she told me what she'd said to him and I did as well. She was my sister again."

"Did she . . ."

Rachel raised a finger to stop before I finished asking.

"Did Sondra have sex with Angelo's daddy? Well not exactly," she said. "When I was in my seventh month village gossip came to me. My sister was telling friends that when she moved back from living in New York she and my guy had been together. She could have told me this before we made a baby, but she didn't. Now she was spreading gossip as though I'd done something sleazy. Sondra needs to put her hands on every guy that's interested in me. I was pissed as hell but at least she was acting like my sister again and the baby was coming."

She paused for a moment to take in the smells and sounds of the night ocean.

"I love it here," she said.

I loved it also. It was such a temptation to stay.

What would become of Rachel in the months and years ahead? Would she leave Angelo behind with her mom and aunt in the summer and go with Sondra and some of the other women to Long Island to harvest marijuana for fast money, maybe meet someone there? I didn't think so. Or would she finally manage to go to medical school in San José, a dream she has held close since she was a kid? I didn't think so. The pull of this place is too powerful. The storms and the rainy season. The memories. Her aunt. The day's menu. She wouldn't need to decide where to go. The weeks and months would pass in a blur. She would watch the tides rising and falling, the bar jacks feeding near the shore, wait for customers. Wait for love to ride into town in a Mercedes. Soon she would be old.

"When Angelo arrived Sondra hardly took notice. She had no interest in being a mom. Maybe it was the smell of the shitty rags I used for diapers," she laughed a little at this. "My sister wasn't made for waking in the night with a screaming baby. She was partying with wealthy guys from New York and Paris. She had that terrific bod and smile. I had my baby sleeping below the bar in the lounge."

The heft of this place was so much bigger and stronger than I was. I could never have survived in Fragata. Sondra never would have allowed it. She'd either fuck me or try to kill me. I'd always be on edge, always an outsider. And Rachel needed her chance to leave the lounge, like her aunt and mom and all the others. She would hate me if I tried to stay.

"Whenever she came here, Sondra walked past Angelo with hardly a glance. 'You never visited Silvano once in the hospital,' she said to me. It was true. Whenever Mommy and

Sondra cried over their pictures of Silvano in his hospital bed
I was never in one of them."

~

Rachel had told me her story. . . . She was stretching, beginning to stand for a goodnight kiss before putting on her lip
gloss. She didn't like lingering goodbyes. I was scrambling
for what to say, to stretch it out with something memorable,
when Sondra came to mind. Another possibility I hadn't considered. Maybe her appearance wasn't staged by Rachel.
Sondra had been stalking us the whole time I'd been here,
watching from the shadows, judging, insinuating herself. But
if this were true, how would her last jarring moment work
best in the story? How would it seem most prescient and
true? Should it happen at the end or close to the beginning,
foreshadowing the entire saga? As if I were writing Rachel's
story in my head. This possibility had been sitting on the shelf
untended for all of these weeks in Fragata. I hadn't wanted to
look, to go back there. But just what if I actually tried to write
the entire crazy quilt story of Silvano, Rachel and Sondra and
Sylvia and the poison and Craig, Sammy Davis Jr. and the rats
and Robert and the hand cream, tried to write it and that would
turn my big deception into something else. Whether I could
pull it off or publish the thing, I didn't know that part. It was
a shame I hadn't used a tape recorder with her or even taken

notes. And my memory wasn't so good anymore. But if I tried to write the pages, it might be enough for her to feel good about the book. Rachel once told me that when I wrote the novel and sent her a copy she'd put it under her pillow. It was such a sweet thing to say, but I had cringed at the depth of my deceit and didn't know how to answer, tried to put it out of my mind. My face turned red each time she mentioned the book. But maybe Rachel could meet me in New York and feel good about being with an exterminator who wrote a book about her after he came home from work. And much better than tape recordings and typed notes I'd have her with me in my little apartment whispering ideas I could never have imagined.

I could help her escape the lounge and maybe we could make it work. It was a big risk getting back to the life I hadn't lived for thirty years, the life that had broken me and had taken me decades to get over so I could feel good about going to the Jets games on Sundays with Robert. Did I dare? Should I? I didn't know if I had it in me to write a decent book . . . or how long it would take. . . . Could I tie it all together, the tragedy of Silvano, the rats and roaches, the tidal wave, while trying to make a life together? Could she be happy in the city? It was a big reach.

But I'd ask her. I thought she'd come. And we'd see.

Acknowledgments

I wouldn't publish anything without first putting it past my wife, Bonnie, and my son, Josh. They are my most enthusiastic and toughest readers. I've worked with many magazine and book editors and often felt like I was in a tug of war, bartering over sentences and sometimes giving away good material that should have remained in the book. Bonnie is the only editor I fully trust. If a sentence of mine is awkward she can fix it without losing my sensibility or the rhythm of my prose. If I lose my way in the narrative she bails me out with ideas that feel like my own. Really, she is a marvel. I could not write a decent book without her.

Josh is a powerful thinker and his ideas have deeply stirred many people, including his dad. Usually he only makes a few remarks about a manuscript of mine but they leave a mark. Josh read an early draft of this book and recognized that my narrator was committing a kind of aesthetic suicide in the opening pages. Honestly, his critique annoyed the hell out of me but after a couple of weeks of brooding I went back and re-conceived the first third of the novel with a whole new energy and direction that persisted all the way through to the end. Thanks, man.

Karol Cabezas Mora told me enchanting stories about life in a small seaside fishing village in Costa Rica, some of which, in altered form, became part of the tapestry of this novel. She brought the customs and mores of her world to life for me. Thanks so much, Karol.

My friend Joel Grassi has three graduate degrees but he makes his living as an exterminator. He has entertained me with stories and written descriptions of harrowing and hilarious adventures dispatching rats and vermin of all types and has allowed me to borrow from his blog and dip into the fantastic material of his life.

Sofia Ruiz is a magnificent Costa Rican painter whose work strays magically from realism into abstraction. She always goes for the story beneath the surface. When I saw her work, I was blown away and reached out to her to ask if she would consider creating images for my novel. After reading *Strange Love* she agreed. I said to her at the start I envisioned her art in juxtaposition to the written page rather than serving as mere illustration. Her images are her own interpretation of characters and events and create an unusual and exciting synergy.

Thank you Nathalie Arias for modeling for Sofia Ruiz's remarkable drawings of Rachel. Nathalie is a friend and one day while I was writing the book I realized that the broad reach of Nathalie's emotions seemed to mirror the changing faces of my character. She was gracious enough to allow us to photograph her for hours.

My friend Aiden Slavin is a terrifically gifted young author. For a half year before I attempted the first paragraph of *Strange Love* he and I met several times at a Village restaurant for spaghetti and red wine while I shared some of the wildly disparate worlds and ideas I wanted to pull together in the new book. In my dreams *Strange Love* made sense but in the light of day the story came unhinged and scared me to death. Aiden's enthusiasm and laughter and insights gave me the confidence to dive into the pool.

I want to give special thanks to Shuman Li. Before she moved to Louisiana to get married and have her baby, we would sometimes meet for coffee and she'd tell me harrowing stories of growing up in China as an eight-year-old, forced to live at home by herself for months on end, feeding herself, dealing with terror and sadness, growing up young, while her parents were off working hundreds of miles away. She is a vivid and nuanced storyteller, better than a lot of folks who make a living at it. Her natural gift inspired my thinking about the character, Rachel, in *Strange Love*.

Thank you, Paul Slavin, for your thoughtful advice about

how to bring this book into the world. Your company has produced the most beautiful looking books for me and made the entire publishing process a delight.

Thank you so much, Chris Begg. You were my earliest reader of *Strange Love*. You were so encouraging and smart and eloquent talking about my first chapters when I was feeling a bit shaky . . . I always enjoy our talks about life and writing, which for me are closely linked.

I always show Melinda Matthews and Bruce Pandolfini early drafts of my books. They are part of my home team, thoughtful insightful readers with editing chops and deep knowledge of literature. Their encouragement and suggestions over the years have been hugely helpful, and especially so with *Strange Love*.

Joe Hannan helps me in so many ways. He is a graceful writer who has a keen sense for the right audience for a book. His marketing advice has been so helpful, and particularly so when matched with his graphic talent. Joe's Facebook and website designs for me have been terrific. Joe and and his talented wife, Frances, shot and edited short videos for *Deep Water Blues* and *Strange Love* that are on point and beautiful to look at. Joe is a great pleasure to work with.

Jay Bergen, thanks for your thoughtful reading of the manuscript. Your guidance and counsel was hugely important and I cannot thank you enough.

ACKNOWLEDGMENTS

Thanks so much Jacob Allgeier for all your advice and assistance taking the manuscript and turning it into a book. Mauricio Díaz, the design work you have done for *Strange Love* is just beautiful.

Fred Waitzkin was born in Cambridge, Massachusetts. His father, Abe, was a salesman and his mother, Stella, an abstract expressionist painter and sculptor. To the best that Waitzkin can recall, his parents never shared a warm moment. Early on, the young Waitzkin considered careers in sales, big-game fishing, and Afro Cuban drumming, but by the age of thirteen he decided he would be a writer. Both of his parents were strong literary influences, along with Ernest Hemingway: "His little sentences thrilled me with descriptions of men pulling in huge sharks and marlin."

Waitzkin was an English major at Kenyon College in Gambier, Ohio. During the summer vacation following his junior year, he met Bonnie on a sword fishing trip, and a year later they were married. Waitzkin received a master's degree at New York University and, for a time, considered pursuing a career as a scholar of seventeenth-century poetry. He taught English at the University of the Virgin Islands; however, he admits that it wasn't his love of teaching poetry that intrigued him about St. Thomas, but rather the rumors of thousand-pound blue marlin that were said to graze twelve or fifteen miles north of the island in a patch of ocean called "the saddle."

Following their St. Thomas years, the Waitzkins settled in

New York City. After collecting a great many magazine rejections for his short stories, Waitzkin began writing feature articles, personal essays, and reviews for numerous publications including *Esquire*, *Forbes*, the *New York Times Magazine*, the *New York Times Book Review*, *New York* magazine, *Outside*, and *Sports Illustrated*.

In 1984, Waitzkin published his memoir, *Searching for Bobby Fischer*, about himself and his son Josh, a chess prodigy. The book became an internationally acclaimed bestseller. In 1993, the film adaptation was released by Paramount Pictures and, that same year, was nominated for an Academy Award.

In 1993, Waitzkin published *Mortal Games*, a biography about world chess champion Garry Kasparov. It has been described as "a remarkable look inside the world of genius—a brilliant exploration of obsession, risk and triumph."

In 2000, he published *The Last Marlin*, a memoir that was selected by the *New York Times* as "a best book of the year."

In the spring of 2013, St. Martin's Press published *The Dream Merchant*, Waitzkin's first novel. *Kirkus Reviews* wrote, "Waitzkin offers a singular and haunting morality tale, sophisticated, literary, and intelligent. Thoroughly entertaining. Deeply imaginative. Highly recommended."

His second novel, *Deep Water Blues*, published in 2019 by Open Road Media, is set on a remote and sparsely populated Bahamian island, where a peaceful marina becomes a battleground. "This is like sitting by a fire with a master storyteller whose true power is in the realm of imagination and magic," wrote Gabriel Byrne.

Waitzkin lives in Manhattan and Martha's Vineyard with his wife, Bonnie, and frequently visits Costa Rica. He has two children, Josh and Katya, and two cherished grandsons, Jack and Charlie.

Sofia Ruiz is a Latin American artist born in San Jose, Costa Rica, in 1982. In 2000, she entered the School of Fine Arts in Costa Rica, majoring in painting and printmaking. She has won many national and international awards. Her work has been shown in France, Italy, Spain, South Korea, Panama, Colombia, Cuba, and the United States, in addition to Costa Rica.

Ruiz's paintings, including many portraits of children, suggest what lies behind an apparent normality. Her characters are often beautiful on the surface, but almost always they are haunted, incomplete, and fractured. We witness them more deeply the longer we look. Ruiz winds the clock forward and we see these beautiful children marked by a painful future.

FRED WAITZKIN

FROM OPEN ROAD MEDIA

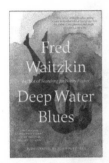

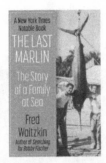

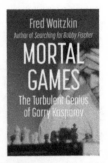

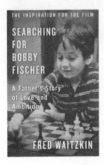

INTEGRATED MEDIA